MINEFIELD

A GABRIEL WOLFE NOVELLA

ANDY MASLEN

TYTON PRESS

This book is dedicated to all the children given education, and hope, by the Ponheary Ly Foundation.

And to Ponheary Ly and Lori Carlson.

"Should a seeker not find a companion who is better or equal, let them resolutely pursue a solitary course."
Siddhārtha Gautama, The Buddha

1

THE FIRST MINE

The grunting cough was too deep to be human. Eli Schochat looked around, trying to ignore the pain in her right leg. At first, she saw nothing. Just the tumbled piles of mossy stone blocks, as if a giant had tired of his construction set and swept the half-finished temple aside. Then she saw it.

Moving with sinuous grace, its spotted flanks rippling, a leopard was creeping towards her, picking its way daintily between the blocks, fixing her with its golden eyes. One forepaw raised, it stilled itself mid-stride, as if turned to the same stone of which the temple had been built so many centuries before. It opened its mouth and cough-grunted again. A distant echo bounced back off the temple walls.

Sunlight filtered onto the forest floor in narrow beams, dappling the low vegetation with paler and darker spots of vivid green. During the night, Eli's ears had become attuned to the many different sounds of the forest: the croaks, chirrups, buzzes and whines; the cries, screams and howls; the soughing of the wind as it disturbed the high canopy. But the leopard must have been hunting elsewhere in the temple complex, because its reverberating call was new to her.

The ex-Khmer Rouge warlord she'd been sent to assassinate had avoided her bullet by sheer fluke. Having waited for him for over a week, living in a hide she'd built on the outskirts of his compound in the far north of Cambodia, the perfect moment had presented itself. She'd lined up the shot, tucking her head in against the stock of her olive-green Accuracy International AW Covert sniper rifle.

But in the fleeting moment between squeezing the trigger and the 7.62mm subsonic round leaving the muzzle, a wild pig had scampered across the flattened red earth of the compound. Win Yah, the warlord, leaned forward to throw something at the creature and the round flew through empty air before burying itself in the fat trunk of a coconut palm.

She'd had no time for a second shot. Picking her way back to her bike through thick and thorny brush, she'd stumbled and trodden on a landmine. One of the millions laid and never mapped by the Americans, the Khmer Rouge and the Vietnamese.

The charge must have been decayed or damaged in some way, because the mine only partially exploded. Her right leg was burnt by the blast and part of the casing tore open the skin of her knee. By the time she came to, she was trussed up like one of the scrawny chickens she'd seen in Siem Reap market. Someone had inexpertly dressed her wound while she was out. Her satellite phone was encrypted, so no use to her captors, but they'd taken it anyway.

Nobody in the compound spoke English. After beating her for a day or so – she'd passed out once or twice – Win Yah made a call on a battered smartphone. Eli found time, and space, to be amused that the case was a vivid metallic pink, like something a Cambodian girl would carry tucked into her jeans pocket. He spoke Russian. He nodded vigorously every few seconds, barking out a high-pitched "Da! Da!" and occasionally giggling.

When the call ended, he looked at her and uttered a short speech in Khmer. He was smiling, revealing a full double row of gold teeth. Speech over, he turned to one of his men, who couldn't have been older than sixteen, and barked out an order. Eli had no Khmer, but she didn't need a translator for the final part of the order. Emitting another of the freakishly high giggles, Win Yah mimed putting a pistol to his head and pulling the trigger. Without speaking another word, he turned on his heel and left.

The soldier, if that's what he was, pulled Eli to her feet and dragged her to a dusty, dented Jeep. Squinting at the sun, she estimated the time to be about 3.00 p.m. She noticed he had her satphone tucked into a pocket on the side of his trousers. He jerked his chin up. *Get in!* Her hands were tied behind her back with rope, but her feet were free, so she clambered aboard and sat heavily on the rear bench seat. He climbed into the driver's seat, started the Jeep and swung out of the compound, throwing up a cloud of red dust. He had a pistol on his hip, an ageing, Russian-made Makarov. He steered with his left hand and rested his right on the pistol's butt, driving Eli to her place of execution.

2

GOD IS MY OATH

Something Win Yah and his young recruit should have known is that if you want to take away and execute an IDF-trained, former Mossad operator, don't leave their legs untied and then sit in front of them.

After an hour's driving, the temple was in sight. *Now!* Eli thought. *When there's somewhere to hole up and call Gabriel.* She braced herself against the seat back, lifted her legs, and scissored them around the driver' neck.

"Stop!" she shouted.

He clearly daren't remove his hands from the steering wheel, as the rutted track was throwing the Jeep around like it was a toy. He stamped on the brake, bringing the Jeep to a sharp stop and stalling the engine, maybe hoping Eli would be thrown forward. Instead she slumped further down and increased the pressure on his throat. His hands were scrabbling at her ankles, trying to break the iron grip that was gradually choking the life out of him. With a sharp twist, Eli saved him the trouble. His neck broke with a loud snap.

Eli jumped down. She backed into the dead man's body and took the knife from his belt. The rope binding her wrists parted easily; the blade was razor-sharp. She dragged the body out of the Jeep, took the Makarov and the satphone, then climbed in behind the wheel. Smiling, she turned the key fully off in the ignition and then cranked it round again. The engine wheezed as the starter motor struggled to turn it over. Then, nothing. Just a rapid clicking from under the bonnet. Swearing, she repeated the sequence with the key. Now the only sound from the Jeep was the occasional *tink* as the exhaust and engine cooled.

"Fuck it!"

The passenger footwell held a plastic jerrycan of water. Enough for a few days if she was careful. She lifted it out, wincing as the movement put pressure on her wounded leg. Turning away, she limped towards the entrance to the temple.

Since then, she'd been repeatedly attempting to make contact with Gabriel Wolfe, her mission partner. At around noon the following day, she got through.

"Eli! Where are you? What happened?"

"I fucked up, that's what happened. I had his evil head in the crosshairs, the air was still: a clear shot. Then this fucking pig distracted him and I missed. They captured me and gave me a beating, then took me off to this fucking remote temple to execute me."

"Clearly, they failed."

"Yup. They're down a man. Just a kid, but you know my feelings on that subject."

"If a kid's got a gun, he's an enemy combatant."

"In one. So, are we going to *natter*," Eli adopted a stagey British accent for this last word, "all fucking day or are you going to come and find me."

"Sure. I'll grab your location from the GPS in the phone. Are you OK for supplies?"

"I have water, but no food. One Makarov with five rounds in the mag."

"OK, I'll get there as fast as I can. Shouldn't be more than an hour. Hold tight."

While she waited for Gabriel, she drifted into a light sleep, despite an insistent throbbing in her right leg that told her infection had set in. Most likely a result of, rather than despite, the rudimentary field dressing the warlord's people had applied. And she'd dreamt. Of home. Not the poky little Victorian terrace house in Shoreditch that The Department had assigned her. *Home*, home. Israel. Jerusalem.

She'd been a little girl again, playing with a toy soldier. It had once been an air hostess Barbie, but she'd cut up one of her father's old uniform shirts and sewn Barbie a set of fatigues. Her father walked into the courtyard at the back of the house with its geraniums and lemon balm plants in wide-bellied, unglazed, terracotta pots. When he saw the remnants of his shirt, he'd shouted at her, then melted as tears dripped from her eyes. He knelt by her side and asked her about the doll.

"And who is this, Eliya?" he asked, using the family's nickname for their only child, Elisheva, *God is my oath*.

"She's *Samal rishon* Barbie, Papa. She's going to fight our enemies."

"A staff sergeant, eh? Well maybe you could teach her an important lesson for all soldiers."

"What's that, Papa?"

"Make sure you truly know who your enemies are, before you go to war with them."

Then he'd tousled her hair, straightened with a volley of pops from his knees and gone inside to find his wife.

When Eli looked back at *Samal rishon* Barbie, she wailed. The doll was missing her left arm and right leg below the knee. Blood was pouring from the snapped-off plastic limbs and the doll's baby-blue eyes and its lipsticked mouth were stretched wide in a soundless scream of agony.

3

161 ROUNDS

Gabriel put the satphone down on the rattan table. The guest house was ten miles from the warlord's complex. They'd chosen it as a base because the proprietors were used to western guests. The fan above his head was spinning fast enough to create a decent downdraught, but even so, the crushing heat outside was making its presence felt. Sweat dripped steadily from his nose and chin however many times he wiped it away.

He looked up at a spot on the wall to his left. The cobalt-blue gecko who'd been there when he arrived was eyeing him. The same length as his hand, the lizard was so still it seemed it might have been painted onto the bare plaster, though he had come back to the room from time to time to find it had changed position.

"OK, Eric," he said, "looks like we need to prep for an extraction."

The gecko sat motionless, apart from the faintest of vibrations from its ribcage.

Gabriel went to the wardrobe and pulled out a canvas holdall, held closed with a brown leather strap. He hoisted it onto the bed, where it settled with a bounce and a series of squeaks from the springs. When he unzipped it, the contents emitted a sharp whiff of metal, cordite and gun oil. He brought out the items within and laid them out in rows on the counterpane.

A Colt M16 assault rifle, fitted with a canvas webbing sling, an underslung M203 40mm grenade launcher and, mounted on the other picatinny rails, a high-power torch and a telescopic scope.

Two spare NATO STANAG 30-round capacity magazines for the M16, which he'd previously loaded.

Six M203 high-explosive grenades.

A Sig Sauer P226 semi-automatic pistol chambered in .357, fitted with a suppressor and a 15-round magazine. Plus a box of 50 rounds and a black nylon holster.

A Böker tactical knife in a black nylon sheath.

A field first-aid kit including trauma scissors, three syringes of morphine and one containing a wide-spectrum intravenous antibiotic, a tourniquet and a QuikClot sponge.

Two 12-hour operational ration packs.

Water purification tablets.

He took each item in turn and inspected it, physically and visually. He field-stripped the firearms, oiled them and reassembled them.

"A hundred and sixty-one rounds, Eric," he said, glancing at the gecko. "It'll have to do."

4

INFECTED

Eli woke and brushed at her cheeks, which were wet. And then she heard the deep rasp of the leopard's hunting call. She picked up the Makarov and racked the slide. At the metallic snap as the slide returned to the battery position, the leopard hissed at her like a domestic cat, its lips fully drawn back, exposing long, yellow fangs. Then it turned away and sprang twelve feet straight up onto a stone ledge carved with hundreds of dancing gods and goddesses.

She reached down to her other side and grabbed a stone from a small stockpile she'd prised from the hard-packed red earth. She threw the stone up at the leopard, prompting it to take a few more steps further from her.

"Scat, you overgrown tabby cat!" she shouted.

It hissed at her in return and disappeared over the trunk of a tree whose roots twined through gaps between the stones like blood vessels between muscles.

The effort of scaring off the leopard had tired her. The heat of the early afternoon sun was fierce, and enclosed by the stone walls as she was, any breeze that was taking the edge of the heat out in the open wasn't reaching her. Her leg was pulsing with a dull throb of pain as if her heart were sending small packets of poison into her thigh with each beat.

She took a swig of water. Thanked God that at least the warlord kept his men well supplied with that, if not food. She felt lightheaded. She raised her head to the heavens, praying for a swift rescue. As she returned her gaze to the carvings on the green-dressed stones, a wave of dizziness passed over her, threatening to turn the lights out. *Nothing to do now but wait, Samal rishon Barbie,* she told herself.

5

TWO OUTFITS

Gabriel stripped off the tropical kit he'd been wearing – a red-and-white, hibiscus-print Hawaiian shirt and red shorts. Eli had shrieked with laughter the first morning he'd appeared at breakfast in his "tourist camo" as they called it.

"Fuck me, Wolfe! What happened? Did you go shopping with your eyes shut?"

Gabriel had pirouetted in front of her, glancing over his right shoulder in a parody of a catwalk model's pout.

"What's the matter, my lady. Don't you like it?"

"You look like a dick. A handsome dick. But still a dick."

Gabriel sat down at the table. Eli was more soberly dressed in a sage-green linen dress.

"OK then, Miss Fashionista," he said. "What would you suggest?"

Eli stuck her lower lip out and touched her fingertip to it.

"Aw, is Gabriel upset 'cos the nasty lady criticised his dress sense?"

He held up his hands in mock surrender.

"No, no, it's fine. You just carry on with the name calling. I'll just sit here pretending to be Barry from Wimbledon enjoying the

Cambodian countryside. You go off and have fun shooting the bad guy."

His over the top acting of a wounded ego was too much for Eli and she'd resumed her giggles before finally subsiding with a huge sigh.

"Oh, God, you make me laugh."

Smiling despite the seriousness of his mission, Gabriel redressed in more suitable clothing. Jungle camouflage trousers and shirt, camo cap and sand-coloured boots. He threaded the webbing belt through the slots of the Sig's holster and the Böker's sheath and cinched it tight. Finally he packed the rest of the gear into a camo-pattern daysack.

He left the guest house in his rented Ford Ranger pickup with the M16 and the daysack in the passenger footwell.

Heading for Eli's GPS coordinates using Google maps on his own smartphone it took him twenty minutes to get to within a mile of the site. As Eli had told him, her location was a ruined Buddhist temple named Jayon Peah.

Down south, in and around Siem Reap, the temples, centred on Angkor Wat, were a honeypot for the hundreds of thousands of tourists who flocked to Cambodia every year. But up here, tucked away on rural land still heavily mined and littered with unexploded cluster munitions left over from the American carpet-bombing, the temples were closed to the public and left to moulder away on their own.

The last five miles had been over rutted and potholed tracks that were little more than flattened areas of forest floor. He'd been told by the proprietors of the guest house that the locals would wait for their cattle to make paths through the forest before venturing outside their known network of roads and village courtyards. Maybe this was one such track, cleared by cows simply looking for a stream or some fresh grazing.

He wondered how many bovine landmine casualties there had been, or whether cows had some innate ability to detect and avoid buried explosives. His spine protested with a sharp jab of pain with each jolting lurch down into and then out of a pothole. After his teeth had clacked together once too often, he swore, pulled over in a wider stretch of track to allow a motorbike or cart to pass, and climbed out.

He jammed his fists into the small of his back and arched over them, turning his face up to the sun and groaning as the muscles and ligaments holding his vertebrae in place creaked and pinged in protest. On the other side of the cab, he opened the door and reached in to retrieve the M16 and the daysack. Settling the latter onto his back and slinging the former over his right shoulder, he set off down the track.

According to the GPS, Eli should be no more than a mile ahead. On a reasonably well-kept road, that would have taken no more than quarter of an hour. On this particular example of rural transportation engineering he felt he should allow at least twenty-five.

As he walked, he pulled out the satphone and called Eli. Her phone rang on and on but she didn't pick up. Gabriel felt a sudden anxiety squirrelling around in his gut.

"Come on, Eli," he said, pulling the phone away from his ear and checking the display. "Stay with me."

6

THE SECOND MINE

By Eli's side, the satphone rang. She didn't answer. Her head lolled forward on her chest, her arms hung limply at her sides, palms uppermost. Her body was struggling to combat the infection that was raging through her bloodstream. The wound on her knee was filling with pus and the stench was attracting insects. Small brown flies were swarming around the dressing, landing from time to time and crawling around the edges of the bandage. Fifty yards away, prowling along a stone rampart, the leopard was staring down at her.

* * *

The temperature had soared during the morning. Gabriel estimated it as approaching forty Celsius. The humidity was intense, too, and the sweat flowed from him in rivulets, salt stinging his eyes. He came to a grove of mango trees, some of whose branches were overhanging the track. The fruit were so ripe they were falling to the ground with soft thumps. On impact, the yellow-skinned fruits split open to reveal golden-yellow flesh. Gabriel stooped to retrieve an undamaged fruit and cut it open with the Böker. As he walked, he slurped the sweet, aromatic flesh down.

Ahead, he caught a flash of grey-white hide covering a set of bony hips. One of the scrawny cattle farmed up here by the local people was wandering along the red-earth track in front of him. It must have heard, or sensed, his approach, because it turned its head to see who was approaching. At the sight of someone so clearly not part of the local ecosystem, the cow took fright.

With a single deep bellow of fear, it rotated through ninety degrees and crashed off into the undergrowth. Gabriel watched it go, wishing he'd been able to somehow give the beast more advance warning. Then, with a flash of light and a loud bang, the cow turned into a spraying cloud of blood and flesh fragments. A piece of one of its lower legs spun past Gabriel's head before bouncing off a banana palm.

Shit! A landmine. I'm sorry. Then, aloud, Gabriel spoke the words taught to him as a child by Master Zhao, his childhood mentor and surrogate father. "I honour your life."

The cow would provide sustenance for hundreds or maybe thousands of forest creatures, from raptors and wild cats to beetles and flies. He consoled himself with the thought that fate had merely decreed that the cow should enter the food chain a little earlier than planned.

He pushed on, the cloying smell of blood and acrid smoke from the mine's TNT charge thick in his nostrils.

After twenty minutes of walking, during which time the track had deteriorated to the point it barely deserved the name, something about the quality of the sounds from the forest made Gabriel stop and listen. The choir of insects was in full song, joined by tootling birds, and unidentifiable cries and calls that might have been frogs, birds or mammals. But there was a faint reverberation to the sound, as if it were bouncing around. *The temple. I must be almost there.*

Wiping the sweat from his face once again, he unshouldered the M16 and pulled back the charging lever. It snapped back, chambering a 5.56mm NATO round. A round that would yaw in soft tissue, the result of its centre of mass being forward of its centre of gravity. Anyone unfortunate enough to be in the way would sustain catastrophic soft tissue injuries as the wobbling bullet wrought its black magic inside them.

A civilian would have begun shouting for their lost partner as soon as the towering edifice of the temple appeared before them. A civilian would have run for the vast stone gateway and jumped over its fallen lintel, which must have crashed to the ground many years earlier.

A civilian would have tired themselves out in the heat, dashing around in a random search for their loved one. But Gabriel Wolfe was not a civilian. Or not in any sense that mattered, beyond the strict legal definition. No, he was not a serving member of Her Majesty's armed forces. He did not wear a uniform. Or not one issued by the Ministry of Defence. But as an operator for The Department, and one with a background in The Parachute Regiment and 22 SAS, his reactions and his behaviour were different.

An old army mantra played in his head on loop: *look for the presence of the abnormal and the absence of the normal.* On patrol in an Afghan village, why are there no children in the street? Normally they'd be playing in the street, maybe kicking an improvised football around or squatting in little groups chattering. No kids might mean IEDs, or an ambush. Is there a car in a pedestrianised area? Could be a car bomb. Or a man in a combat jacket and jeans in a financial district? It might mean nothing. It might mean he's a suicide bomber. You go carefully, and you stay alert.

So Gabriel stopped walking. He took a water bottle from his daysack and drank half of it. Then he scanned the area in front of him. If he'd been a tourist, he'd have gasped in wonder.

In front of him, smothered with creepers and overhung with tall trees that drooped over its collapsed walls as if exhausted by the heat, an ancient temple loomed. To each side of the massive stone entrance, carved lions twice as tall as a man stood guard. Their mouths grimaced, cheeks pulled back to reveal a double row of pointed teeth. The path, paved with uneven flagstones, led between them and on for a hundred yards to the main body of the temple.

He looked along the path, saw nothing. Checked left and right, again, nothing. Behind him and above, still just him and the millions of insects, birds and animals treating the place as their private sanctuary. Or killing ground.

He stepped over the fallen lintel that partially covered the threshold – a flat stone bar between the lions' feet. In Buddhist culture, to tread on it was considered unlucky. And right now, Gabriel felt he needed all the help he could get.

As he walked onwards, he raised the satphone to his ear and called Eli again. No answer. He let it ring and held it by his side. He strained to catch the ringing sound of her unit that would tell him she was close. He held his breath and closed his eyes, then exhaled slowly through his open mouth, feeling the warm moist air leave his lungs. *Come on, Eli.*

Was that it! He'd heard a faint *de-de-de-de-de-de-de-* that might be the distinctive ringing of the military-issue satphones. But then, he reasoned, it could just as easily be a bird, or even a frog, calling for a mate, or warning others off its territory.

He repacked the phone and walked on, M16 held across his body.

Everywhere he looked, he saw huge piles of cuboid stone blocks. The walls had collapsed or, he supposed, the Khmer Rouge had smashed them down in pursuit of their obscene idea of creating a pure, Marxist Cambodia in "Year Zero".

Mother Nature was playing her part in transforming order into chaos. Trees grew on narrow ramparts, their roots stretching down through clear air until they reached the red earth and burrowed deep in search of water, or squeezing between stones until they forced them apart, to tumble onto the piles of their fellows waiting for them on the ground.

Reaching a small rectangular clearing, bordered on three sides by thirty-foot walls carved with dancing gods and goddesses, he unshouldered his daysack and laid the rifle beside it. Sun was streaming into the central space, illuminating patches of vivid green vegetation, bright with scarlet and yellow flowers.

He turned through 360 degrees, looking high and then low, searching for a hiding place where he might find Eli. He wasn't ready to admit it to himself, but there was every chance she was already dead. From dehydration, a wound, a fall or even from a bite from some local creepy crawly. He looked down at the satphone. Was it worth one more try?

7

PRETTY PUSSY-CAT

Eli enjoyed being free of her earthly body. From her vantage point high above the ground, she looked down at her slumped form. The bandage around her knee had turned a disgusting yellow-brown, and it stank. She could smell it from here. Pus. Decay. Rot. Her trouser leg was stained a deep red from the blood. Around her, brightly coloured birds and butterflies fluttered and swirled, encouraging her to join them. *I'm not ready*, she thought. *Not yet. Let me spend some more time with him.*

A giant butterfly the size of her two outspread hands, its wings an iridescent blue, landed on a carved monkey beside her. It opened its mouth and emitted a loud electronic peeping. Then it spoke.

"You'll have to fight, then, Eli. The odds are stacked against him."

"I will. If I can."

"Then go back. He's calling you."

It emitted the electronic sound again.

De-de-de-de-de-de-de-de-de-de-

Eli opened her eyes to find herself slumped painfully against a stone block, her neck bent at an unnatural angle. The satphone by her left hip was ringing. She snatched it up.

"Gabriel?"

"Oh, thank God. When you didn't answer, I thought —"

"I'm here. I'm OK. Come and get me."

"Where?"

"It's like a walled garden. I don't know where, exactly. Wait! I have a pistol. I'll fire a shot. Try and get a fix."

"OK. Ready."

Eli picked up the Makarov. As she did so, she noticed the leopard watching her from no further than twenty feet away. *Don't make me kill you, pussy-cat*, she thought. *You're much too pretty*. Perhaps sensing that the black object in her hand might give her an advantage over its teeth and claws, the leopard retreated ten feet. Then it turned, leapt onto a fallen tree and scooted up its tilted trunk to the safety of a stone tower carved with enormous Buddha faces.

Aiming vertically, she fired once, wincing as the report intensified her headache, which had been building steadily for the past few hours. Breathing in the sharp smell of the cheap Russian gunpowder, she raised the satphone to her ear again.

"Did you hear me?" she asked.

"I think they heard you back in Siem Reap," Gabriel answered. "I'm on my way. Hold on."

* * *

The gunshot was monstrously loud in the hard acoustics of the temple. It had come, Gabriel estimated, from somewhere to his left. He picked up his daysack and the M16 and set off at a fast walk. He was drenched in sweat and his eyes were stinging from the salt.

He reached a low wall, clambered onto the top and then made his way up one of the sloping piles of stone blocks to a higher rampart. He had to negotiate several twisting roots the thickness of his arm that coiled their way across, around and through the gigantic cubes of greenish-grey stone.

Reaching the top, he cupped his hands around his mouth and called out.

"Eli! Can you hear me?"

Straightaway she answered him and his heart leapt.

"I'm over here."

He looked down and saw her immediately. She was lying with her back against a wall and waving feebly, her hand raised only a little way above her elbow.

Going as fast as he dared, he descended the jumbled pile of stones on the other side of the wall. Jumping down from the final block, he made his way to her across the flat quadrangle of tramped-flat earth. He knelt beside her and grabbed her in a fierce hug, before releasing her.

"How are you? What happened to your leg?"

She smiled weakly up at him.

"I stepped on a landmine. It was faulty. I think only the detonator went off, or a partial charge, but I'm burnt and my knee was laid open."

"OK, let's have a look."

"What time is it?"

"It's one fifteen. Now, hold still."

Gabriel drew his knife and cut away the stained, stinking bandage from her knee. He wrinkled his nose as the strip of grubby cotton fabric came free. The wound was filled with bloody pus, its edges red and puffy.

"That's badly infected. I need to clean it and redress it. I've got some stuff in my med kit that'll help with the pain."

He used some water from his canteen to clean out the wound, trying to ignore Eli's whimper of pain. Next he injected her with the antibiotic and followed the shot with a second syringe of morphine.

Eli sighed as the needle went in.

"Oh, man, that feels good. I hope you've got plenty more in there, doc."

Gabriel smiled.

"Enough to keep you going till we get you back to base."

"Listen, there's a biggish cat stalking around, a leopard, I think. It's been sniffing around, getting cockier. I don't want to kill it but you need to do something or we're going to have to."

Gabriel thought back to the dead cow.

"OK. I think I can distract it long enough for us to exfil." He handed her the M16. "Take this. It's nice and loud and you'll be able to scare it off if it comes back before I do."

"Where are you going?"

"Butcher's shop to get some cat food."

She furrowed her brow.

Leaving her with the canteen of water, he stood and drew his Sig. He made his way back the way he'd come until he reached the site of the cow's untimely demise. He took a bearing on one of the more manageable pieces of the carcass. Then, after holstering the Sig, he broke off a branch from a nearby sapling and started sweeping a path clear through the fallen leaves and forest debris. The chances of there being another mine between the main path and the one that had killed the cow were slim. But slim or not, that still meant he could join it in the low-hanging branches as more food for vultures.

Sweeping methodically from left to right and back again, Gabriel cleared away everything that littered the ground for a couple of feet in front of him. Then, using the other end of the broken branch, he scribbled the top layer of sandy earth away, heart thumping in his chest, butterflies swarming in his gut. On his knees, he leaned over to inspect the ground. He could see no raised detonators. No pins, rings, plates or plungers. He advanced two feet. Repeated the process. Crawled ahead again.

He was just about to place his right knee down when the dry earth a few inches further forward started funnelling down into a regularly shaped depression, almost as if it were running through an oversized egg timer.

8

HALF A HINDQUARTER

There must have been an air gap beneath the mine. The sweeping had disturbed the delicate equilibrium around it and allowed the dry earth covering the detonator to trickle down. Gabriel stopped dead. His knee hovered just a couple of inches above the ground, then moved back. He realised he'd been holding his breath, and let it out in a controlled sigh.

Standing just proud of the dusty red earth was a black plastic disc, from which four stubby arms protruded, north, south, east and west. Gabriel leaned forwards and blew. The detonator was revealed in all its malevolent glory, set into a black plastic disc and enclosed in a green steel ring: the top of the mine casing.

Gabriel had studied mines as part of his SAS training. He recognised this model. It was a Russian PMN 2 anti-personnel mine. Small enough to fit on the palm of a man's hand and containing a tiny amount of TNT – just 115 grammes. Yet subject it to anything above five kilos of pressure and it would explode with enough force to mutilate or kill. Cows, soldiers, pregnant women, children, farmers, doctors, engineers, teachers: mines were indiscriminate killers.

Left behind in their millions by the Americans, the Khmer

Rouge and, finally, the North Vietnamese, the mines were still killing and maiming Cambodians in their thousands. But at least this one wouldn't be adding to the grotesque tally of amputees. Pulling out the Böker, Gabriel dug the mine out. He moved it to one side then made it, without any further incident, to the chunk of bloody flesh and bone he'd fixed on.

He retrieved the meat – a section of the animal's hindquarter by the look of it – and started dragging it back along his mine-free trail, pausing briefly to collect the mine. Shuffling backwards on his knees and elbows, it took more than five minutes to regain the safety of the main path. By the time he got there, his face was running with sweat. He could feel his shirt sticking to his chest and the skin between his shoulder blades.

He stood up and made his way back to Eli, partial cow hindquarter swinging from one hand, mine gripped in the other.

"What have you got there?" she asked.

He explained about the meat and then showed her the mine.

"Wow! OK. That was stupid. I mean super-courageous," she said with a grin. "By the way, whatever you gave me in that syringe? You should be selling it on Pub Street in Siem Reap. Those backpackers would empty their wallets for you."

"Yeah, I bet they would," Gabriel said, inwardly delighted that Eli seemed to have regained some of her old spirit. Her cheeks were still flaring with spots of high colour. But her eyes were clear and she was focusing much better than she had been when he'd first arrived.

"Where's the leopard?" he asked.

"It's been coming from that high wall over there," Eli said, pointing to a pile of stones that filled in the angle between the temple floor and a wall about seventy feet to their west.

Gabriel picked up the hunk of meat and walked to the wall. He took a few paces back then swung his right arm like a pendulum a few times and hurled the ragged meat over the wall. He jogged back to Eli.

"That should fill its belly and keep it happy while we get out of here," he said. "Even apex predators will always choose an easy dead meal over a chancy live one."

"OK, Mister Wildlife Expert. I believe you. Now, are you going to get us out of here or were you thinking of setting up home?"

9

THE MAKING OF A KILLER

"It's too hot to move," Gabriel said. "With your leg infected like that, It'll drain too much of your strength. Let's hunker down here and let you recover. I brought some field rations. We can keep you medicated to damp down your fever and then go this evening. Early. Maybe six or seven. It'll be cooler then and we can make our way back to the truck."

The fact that Eli didn't protest made Gabriel realise how much of an effort she was putting into maintaining her sarcastic attitude. He made her drink more water then settled next to her, the M16 across his lap. They were in shade and the heat was bearable if they kept still. Eli leaned against him and was soon asleep, snoring quietly.

A deep coughing grunt brought Gabriel back to high alertness. *Definitely a leopard*, he thought. *That jungle warfare course was the best value for money ever.* As the grunt rumbled and echoed through the temple, he thought back to a sunlit classroom at MOD Catterick, motes of dust illuminated in mid-air. He and a dozen other Special Forces operators had listened attentively as the instructor ran through a set of slides of predators, scavengers and, as he called them, "the nasty little buggers who won't kill you, but will seriously fuck up your day". The tall infantry officer, a Major Mark Finlay, had played audio of the calls and cries of everything from big cats to birds of prey.

The coughs subsided, first to a loud purring, almost like an engine idling, then to silence. Gabriel visualised the big cat dragging the lump of dead cow away to a lair somewhere, preferably on the other side of the temple complex. *Excellent*, he thought. *Now the coast's clear all we have to do is wait for evening and get out of here.* He let his eyes close.

* * *

Win Yah was ruminating on Samang's absence. A few hours he might have put down to his man having some fun with the woman before killing her. Maybe finding a roadside stand and treating himself to a skinful of Angkor beers. Then sleeping it off until the morning. But it was now after two in the afternoon: almost a day since he'd sent him to kill the woman. That meant trouble. That meant he needed to investigate. He called his second-in-command, a wiry, dark-skinned man called Lon Sen.

"Samang's not back. We need that Jeep. And the woman's satellite phone could be useful, too. Go and get two men, then come with me. We'll go to the temple and see what's happened to that idiot boy."

The quartet armed themselves with AK-47s, loaded a spare jerrycan of gas onto a rack on the back of a second Jeep, then scorched out of the compound, throwing out red grit and dust in a drifting cloud.

Win Yah had not, originally, been a killer. Or even a particularly violent man. He had been born in a village northeast of Siem Reap. He made his living tending a small market garden, just a quarter of a hectare, in which he used to grow mangoes, tomatoes and squash, which his wife used to sell at the market.

Then, one day, a group of thirty Khmer Rouge had crashed into the village armed with Soviet-made assault rifles and pistols. The man at their head had stood on the bonnet of his Chinese-made armoured car and announced through a megaphone that as of now, they were all members of the Khmer Rouge. Their duty to Brother Number One was to assist him in his transformation of the corrupt, imperialist, capitalist kingdom of Cambodia into Democratic Kampuchea.

He would always remember the date: April 17th 1975.

Two weeks later he killed his first human being. The man was a schoolteacher. He had pleaded for his life on his knees, but Win Yah had pulled the trigger anyway. Better that than receiving a bullet in the back of his own head. Over the next six months, he multiplied that single corpse into a mountain of corpses. In the end, he'd killed so many people — men, women, children, even babies — that he lost count. He lost his humanity, too, sloughing off all compassion, empathy and loving kindness as enjoined by the Buddha, until all that was left was a husk, like the shed exoskeletons of dragonfly larvae that clung to reeds poking out of the Tonlé Sap river.

Through his zealotry, he avoided the fate of so many of the Khmer Rouge cadres, falling first under suspicion of treason and then under the blows of their newly recruited comrades. He even murdered his own wife, when the new lists of traitors were issued, feeling nothing as he stove in her skull with the butt of his AK-47.

When the Vietnamese invaded in '79, ending Pol Pot's murderous reign of terror, Win Yah had headed north, fearing recriminations. There, he established a new life for himself as a warlord, first taking over a village and then offering "protection" to local businesses and conducting a lucrative trade in heroin smuggling across the border with Thailand.

When he discovered that the heroin route was part of a bigger and more complex racket involving financing Islamist terror groups, he'd simply renegotiated his fee. Upwards. And if his men occasionally needed to blow off steam by travelling to a nearby town or village and raping a few of the women and girls, or maiming their husbands with machetes, well, it was better than what their parents' generation had dealt with so they should, on the whole, count their blessings.

And now the killer was sitting behind the wheel of an American Jeep, jouncing along an unmetalled road with his trusted lieutenant Lon Sen by his side and two more hardened killers behind them. They wanted their other Jeep back, and the satphone. And they wanted to know what that hapless idiot Samang had got himself into.

"He probably went off and got drunk," Lon Sen said. "Fucked her, killed her, then celebrated too hard."

"If he did I'll celebrate his fucking head with a rifle butt," Win Yah said in a low, dangerous voice.

The drive had taken almost a hour and his back was complaining. He let the narrow rim of the steering wheel run through his hands as the front wheels hopped into and out of ruts and potholes that threw the four men left and right like rag dolls. Easing off the gas, he brought the Jeep round a sharp bend and then swore.

"Shit! Look. That's our Jeep."

"And that's Samang," Lon Sen added, pointing through the windscreen at the supine corpse of the twenty-year-old fighter who wouldn't be celebrating anything ever again.

The four men climbed out of their Jeep and approached Samang's body. Flies were already swarming over his ears, eyes, nostrils and lips. Win Yah poked the toe of his boot at the head, which lay at an unnatural angle. It flopped over sideways, creaking loudly, so that the face hit the red dirt.

Lon Sen scratched the top of his head.

"She did that?"

"Who else, idiot?" Win Yah shouted, making the older man flinch.

The two subordinates exchanged a quick glance, though neither cracked a smile. They'd seen their boss summarily execute men for less.

Win Yah looked closely at the ground around the Jeep, making a complete circuit.

"Right. She must be in there somewhere. No footprints except for a single set leading into the temple. Get your AKs!"

10

HYPERVIGILANCE

Gabriel woke from a dream in which he'd been drinking from a young, green coconut, sucking the cool, refreshing liquid inside through a straw. His shirt was soaked in sweat and his tongue was stuck to the roof of his mouth. He scanned the area in front of them and the ramparts that loomed over them. No big cat. Good. Maybe the unexpected bounty of a few kilos of fresh beef had satisfied it and it had gone off to sleep somewhere.

He looked right to check on Eli. At some point she had shifted position and was now lolling back against the wall, her head on one side. He placed his lips to her forehead. She was hot, but it was the heat of skin cooling its owner down, not the blaze of a fever. The time was 3.15 p.m., still several hours before they could leave.

How anyone could have conceived of building such an ornate structure so deep in the forest baffled him. Who would see it? Was it a priest-cult, its leaders so revered that they could command a slave army to build whatever they told them to, wherever they chose? He knew Angkor Wat, the vast complex of temples outside Siem Reap, had been built in just 30 years. It occupied a space into which you could have fitted a small city. It seemed Buddhists weren't any more averse to a bit of architectural grandstanding than the cathedral-, mosque-, temple- and synagogue-builders of the time.

Trying to calculate how many men would be needed to move just a single one of the vast stone blocks, he almost missed the high-pitched giggle that rose above the uniform background sizzle of insects. His conscious mind ignored it. But somewhere deep in his unconscious mind — the mind that every seasoned soldier develops, the mind some call their "spider sense", and others "hypervigilance" — an alarm bell rang. It increased in volume until Gabriel took notice. At which point the hairs on his forearms and the back of his neck stood on end, thousands of minuscule muscles tugging the follicles erect. A useless effect on a hairless ape, but one that in bygone times would have made Gabriel appear bigger to an enemy.

11

EVERYONE'S FRIGHTENED OF SOMETHING

Slowly, he lifted the M16 from his lap and curled his right hand around the pistol grip, keeping his index finger straight along the outside of the trigger guard. For now. He breathed shallowly through his mouth and waited. Straining to catch that oddly childlike sound again.

He didn't have to wait long.

He jumped to his feet. Turned and looked down at Eli, who was still sleeping. He leant the M16 against the wall then crouched and shook her shoulder, simultaneously placing his free hand over her mouth. Her eyes opened slowly then popped wide as she felt his palm against her lips. He mimed a shushing sound then lifted his hand from her face.

Leaning close, he whispered into her ear.

"I heard something. It sounded like a man, giggling."

"Tourist?" she whispered back.

He shook his head.

"Out here? No. Something's up."

"I guess it could be Win Yah, or one of his men. Maybe they came looking for the guy who drove me out here."

Gabriel nodded.

"OK. I'm going to take a look around. Take my Sig." He handed over the pistol and the box of ammunition.

She took the gun by the grip. Ejected the magazine and checked the spring pressure, then reseated it in the butt. Before he left, Gabriel cut down a couple of palm fronds and laid them across Eli's left leg and her torso as basic camouflage.

Holding the M16 across his body, index finger still mounted across the side of the trigger guard, Gabriel made his way to the nearest wall and began climbing, pausing briefly to sling the rifle over his back. Feeling for a handhold, he inserted his fingers into a deep crack between two stones and felt something move beneath his questing fingertips. He adjusted his grip and was about to put his weight on the hand when two, three and then four fat, hairy, brown legs emerged in slow motion from the gap between the stones.

He jerked his hand back as the tarantula emerged, fixed him with a baleful glare from its eight beady little black eyes and moved away in a laborious series of movements that had Gabriel's heart thumping like a drum in his chest. Gabriel Wolfe – Special Forces veteran, winner of the Military Cross for gallantry, government assassin, unnecessary risk-taker – hated spiders.

Once the malignant arachnid had moved away, he resumed his ascent of the pyramidal pile of stones, gaining the relatively safety of the top of the wall in a few more minutes. He lay prone on the rampart and surveyed the temple floor beyond its further side. A brief flash of light a hundred yards distant caught his eye. He zeroed in on the spot and waited, breathing shallowly.

There it was again! The sun was glinting off something shiny – metal, maybe, or glass. He unslung the M16, brought it up to his shoulder and sighted through the scope. In a slow, deliberate movement, he swept the rifle from left to right. He concentrated on the magnified circle presented by the scope, straining to discern anything that might indicate a threat, or, less likely, the possibility of rescue.

Shit! Company. The wrong kind of company.

12

JUMP OR DIE

Through the scope, Gabriel could see two short, brown-skinned men walking into the temple through the main entrance. He recognised neither man, but their motley collection of camouflage and khaki garments marked them out as members of Win Yah's crew of bandits. That and the AK-47s they were carrying. They were scanning the ground in front of them and gesturing vigorously. Arguing, maybe, or just discussing how they would deal with Eli when they found her. The man on the left threw back his head and let out a piercing giggle that reached Gabriel a split-second later. OK, so not arguing. Great. Now what?

He briefly considered lighting them up with a sustained burst from the M16. And just as quickly dismissed it. If they'd brought company, Gabriel would only succeed in alerting the rest of them, even if he'd reduced their numbers in the process. Instead, he shouldered the rifle and began working his way along the rampart, aiming to get behind them, where he would use the Böker.

The heat and humidity were stifling. He swiped a hand across his brow and continued his crouching progress over the uneven paved walkway. He kept the two bandits in view: they were walking into the central space of the temple, still chatting, occasionally pointing at a statue and giggling.

He'd begun to plan his attack on the two men when his train of thought was derailed by a gap in the rampart. No more than six feet, but it was a forty-foot drop to the ground. It was immediately apparent what had caused the breach. Wedged about halfway down the crevasse, a huge silver-barked tree lay at a forty-five degree angle. It must have toppled during a storm. Or perhaps the Khmer Rouge had taken offence to a monument celebrating a deity other then Pol Pot. On the other side of the gap, Gabriel could see relatively even slabs, though they were green with algae, a result of being situated in the shade of a second broad-leafed tree.

Pausing only for the briefest of moments to collect his thoughts and ensure his rifle was secure across his shoulders, he measured out three paces back, then bent forward at the waist, took a deep breath and ran.

The jump should have been an easy one. Certainly no more difficult than that which Gabriel and three fellow soldiers had mastered during their SAS selection week. It was a five-foot gap between the Isle of Barra in the Outer Hebrides and a basalt column nicknamed Old Tom, which had been split from the cliff by erosion. Then, failure meant a drop of hundreds of feet into the North Sea or onto the jagged blades of rock spearing out of the water.

As Gabriel reached the lip of the drop, he planted his left boot and bent at the knee ready to launch himself across. But instead of getting a clean contact and propelling himself up and over the gap, he hit a patch of moss and lost traction.

The jump was a disaster; with his left leg already falling away, his right swung up uselessly, already heading for the broken face of the wall opposite. He slammed into the edge of the rampart, driving the wind from his lungs with a grunt, and scrabbled for grip on the top edge. And at first he thought he'd made it.

His fingers dug into a crack between two of the slabs. Ignoring the pain, he dug them in deeper and took his weight on his hands, beginning to heave himself up and over onto his belly. With a grating noise, the slab slipped towards him, dropping him back over the edge. Panicking, he kicked his booted feet into the side of the wall, desperately searching for a toehold. Then he was falling.

13

TUNNEL RAT

Gabriel rotated in the air half a turn before slamming down, face-first onto the sloping trunk of the fallen tree. In the distance he heard one of the two bandits call out. He couldn't understand the words, but their implication was clear as day.

"That way!"

His chest was aching and each inhalation brought a sharp stabbing sensation under his right armpit. But this was no time for giving in to pain. He needed to move. Clinging to the smooth bark like a monkey to its mother's belly, he shuffled his way to the ground as fast as he could. The tree had no branches below those that had partially demolished the wall, and his progress was unimpeded.

It took him ten seconds or so to reach terra firma, and as soon as his boots touched the dry red earth, he turned and ran for cover: a dark doorway in the centre of a massive stone wall, flanked with more carved lions. Once inside the pitch-dark space, he felt his way along, fighting to get his breath under control. His questing fingers found an alcove, perhaps twice as deep as a man's torso was wide, and he pushed inside the narrow space.

From outside he could hear the two bandits shouting to each other. In his mind, the dialogue went:

"Have you found him yet?"

"No! He's not here."

"Well, keep looking. He can't have got far."

Gabriel drew the Böker from its sheath. He reversed his grip so the point was uppermost. No stranger to knife-fighting, he relaxed a little as he gripped the hilt tight in his fist. Not so long ago he'd been engaged in a fight to the death with a rogue CIA agent in one of Cambodia's killing fields. He was ready to add a couple more kills to his tally.

He bent at the hip and felt on the ground by his left boot. His fingers closed on a pebble. Squatting, he drew his left arm back and tossed the pebble out of the tunnel entrance. It landed on the stones outside and bounced along with a series of clicks.

The ruse worked. Gabriel heard a shout. Then the sound of booted feet coming closer, and the charging lever on an AK-47 being pulled back and let fly with a loud *clack*. He flattened himself against the rear wall of the alcove in a crouch, gripped the Böker a little tighter and waited.

The light at the entrance dimmed, then darkened, as a human form blocked the rectangular opening. Outlined as a stark silhouette, it was clearly one of Win Yah's men. The distinctive shape of the AK's barrel and front sight made that abundantly clear. The man lowered his rifle into a ready to fire position, holding the hand guard and pistol grip.

Gabriel slowed his breathing and allowed his pulse to settle. No sense in missing your mark because there's too much adrenaline in your system. He felt a familiar calm settle over him. At times, after the wetwork was done and he was relaxing with a drink, he'd ponder the meaning of this state of mind. How had he got to this ... ease, with killing? But now? Contacted by the enemy? No. Philosophy was as much use as a rubber bayonet.

Gabriel waited in his crouch. His vision had improved just enough in the dark space to make out the shape of the approaching bandit. His man, on the other hand, would have pupils the size of pinheads after the bright sunshine outside. They'd be struggling to widen fast enough to let in precious photons. And the bright, white rectangle at the far end of the tunnel wouldn't be helping either.

The air smelled of damp stone, earth and the approaching man's body odour. Gabriel sank even further into himself as the man passed in front of his hiding place. Gabriel straightened, moved on silent feet out of the alcove, and pounced.

He yanked the man's head over with his left hand and brought the knife forward in a vicious, upwards thrust that penetrated the man's side, just below his ribcage. Gabriel turned into the thrust, using his hip to develop extra power, and drove the tip of the knife into the visceral organs. He pulled it free and stabbed again, this time around the front, and into the heart. The man's struggles subsided in seconds as the damaged heart pumped his lifeblood outwards over Gabriel's right hand and forearm; and inwards, filling his body cavity. He sagged, and Gabriel withdrew his blade, letting the man crumple at his feet.

Gabriel wiped the knife clean on the fallen man's shirt and sheathed it. He collected the AK and a belt-mounted pistol and retraced his steps to the tunnel entrance. Blinking in the sunshine, he removed the AK's magazine and pocketed it, then dropped the now useless rifle into a water-filled stone basin about seven feet to a side. The rifle made a loud splash as it landed then sank below the surface. He stuck the pistol, a Makarov, into the back of his waistband. *One down*, he thought. *But how many to go?*

45

14

M203

A yell and a burst of automatic fire provided an answer. *At least one.* He dived behind a huge carved cylinder as bullets whined past his ears and chips of stone flew out from its curved surface.

The man was undisciplined. He was firing indiscriminately instead of waiting for his target to reappear. Gabriel unshouldered his M16 and set the fire selector switch to BURST. *Seeing as you already know I'm here.* He loaded a high explosive grenade into the M203 then held the rifle up over his head and pulled the launcher's trigger. The recoil pushed the rifle back against Gabriel's extended arms, but that was fine. He wasn't going for pinpoint accuracy.

With a loud bang, the grenade exploded. Gabriel didn't hesitate. Pulling the stock into his shoulder, he swung the barrel up and over the top of the cylinder and fired two bursts in quick succession. He saw the bandit scurrying for cover, firing from the hip as he ran. Leading his man by a couple of feet, Gabriel fired a third burst, hitting the bandit in the chest. The man screamed and pitched forward, rolling onto his side and losing his grip on the AK.

Gabriel vaulted over the stone cylinder and strode over to the fallen bandit. He was struggling to release a pistol from a holster on his belt, but the blood soaking the front of his shirt told Gabriel he was never going to drag it free. Five feet from his man, he brought the M16 up to his shoulder, took aim, and killed him with a double tap to the head. Another AK, another magazine. Gabriel retraced his steps and dropped the rifle into the basin and added the magazine to his already bulging pocket.

Something salty stung his eye. More sweat, he thought, bringing his hand up to wipe his forehead. His palm came away wet, but with blood not sweat. Maybe one of the stone chips from the fallen column had cut him as it spun out under the impact of the AK round. It wasn't sheeting down, so just a scratch. Gabriel willed himself to breathe steadily and closed his eyes.

He strained to catch a sound other than the symphony of shrill cries, metallic buzzes and birdsong. No voices, this time. No giggles, shouts or screams. No gunfire. So they hadn't found Eli yet. He needed to hurry. The Israeli was a good shot but she was fighting an infection and her leg wound would hamper any attempt to run or find a better hiding place. He needed to hurry.

Climbing back up to the rampart, he heard the cough-grunt that had punctuated the afternoon. The leopard was back.

He flattened himself onto the paved walkway and used the M16's scope to survey the area in front of him. He saw only tumbled stones, leaning trees and the thick, scrubby vegetation that lay between him and Eli. No lithe quadruped with tawny mottled flanks and three-inch long canines. No skinny bipeds with khaki battledress and yard-long AK-47s. He climbed down on the far side of the wall and, keeping to the perimeter of the roughly square arena bounded by the ramparts, made his way as quickly as he dared back towards Eli.

The distinctive sound of a Sig Sauer pistol being fired sent his heart into overdrive.

Three shots in quick succession.

A gap, then a single shot.

A burst of automatic fire easily recognisable as a AK-47.
A double-tap.
Gabriel's mind locked up for a second.
Eli!

15

P226

From her makeshift shelter, Eli listened to the sounds of a firefight, desperate to support Gabriel. She tried rolling onto her side in preparation for standing and had to bite back a scream as the agony of her swollen and infected knee made her topple sideways. *Fuck it, Eli Schochat. You're no use to him down here. Think!*

She didn't have time to formulate anything beyond that initial instruction to her clouded brain. Strolling down a stone-flagged path, an AK-47 held across his body, was a man in combat gear. He was darker-skinned than other Cambodians, taller too.

OK. Let's even up the odds, Eli thought, not knowing what they'd been originally, nor that Gabriel had already made them two to two. The man was sixty yards away. Too far for a kill shot even for a pistol markswoman without a raging fever. But for Eli, he might as well have been a mile distant. Gritting her teeth, she waited for him to draw closer, praying that he wouldn't see her beneath her covering of palm fronds.

Fifty yards.

Eli raises the Sig in a two-handed shooter's grip.

Forty five.

She brings the barrel up until she can sight along it, aligning the iron sights on the man's head.

Forty.

She takes up first pressure on the trigger.

Her arm wobbles. Her vision blurs.

She shakes her head, which sends it spinning.

"Come on, Eliya," she hears Papa saying. "You can do it."

She aims centre-mass and squeezes off three shots.

BANG-BANG-BANG

The sharp tang of the gunsmoke clears her head for a moment. Did I hit him? Yes! He's on the ground. Prone. No! He's rolling to one side. Her perception of time has been knocked for a loop by whatever Gabriel injected into her muscle. He's moving in slow motion.

She aims again and fires. A single shot this time. Hopeless! The bullet ricochets off the stonework miles to the man's right with a screaming whine and disappears into the trees.

Now Win Yah's man is shooting back. One burst after another. His 7.62mm rounds are slamming into the walls and the columns around her. *He's spraying the bullets like a kid with a hosepipe*, she has time to think. *Maybe he's never fired an AK before. He must have done. But he looks kind of young. Child soldier?* Eli finds she is conducting this internal conversation with herself while preparing to put her man down. By an immense effort of will, she throws off the muzzy feeling and doubled imagery in front of her and raises her pistol once more.

She feels tired. Exhausted. The noise from the AK is deafening but it helps her focus. She sights on his head and pulls the trigger. A double-tap. She misses. Squeezes the trigger again. The gun jams. *Oh fuck, please! Not now.* Her fingers struggle to perform the simple routine to clear a jam, drummed into her by her IDF firearms instructors so many years before. But they are fat and rubbery and refuse to obey her.

She looks up. The man is standing. Grinning. He has gold teeth. They glint in the sun. He has dropped out the magazine from his AK and casually brings out a new one from a pouch at his belt and slams it home.

He stands ten feet away and says something to her in Khmer. She's learnt a few words. The usual social lubricants: please – *som*; thank you – *ah-koon*; hello – *sus'aday*; goodbye – *leah hi*. But no more than that. It's a hard language. The alphabet is no help. A bit like Hebrew. Squiggles and dots. She imagines he's giving her a speech about how she shouldn't have ventured into Win Yah's kingdom. How she's about to meet her ancestors. Or maybe, given the leering expression, how he's going to fuck her before he kills her.

Suddenly she's tired. The gun, *fucking useless gun*, won't clear. She tries to throw it at him but her arm is made of lead and it falls a couple of feet from her right boot. He laughs. Points his AK at her midriff.

And then he flies sideways in a blur of yellow and black.

He is screaming as the leopard fastens its long fangs into the soft flesh of his throat. As it bites down, the scream is choked off as if someone has hit a mute button. The AK flies from his hands as the big cat attacks and now his empty hands are scrabbling at the beast's mottled flanks. The leopard shakes its head, once. Eli hears, quite clearly, the snap as the man's cervical vertebrae part company, severing his spinal cord. Her heart is racing. The leopard turns its head to regard her with eyes the colour of liquid gold. At no point does it loosen its grip on the man's throat. Bright, arterial blood is spurting out from the deep wounds in his neck and staining the greyish-white fur of the cat's throat red.

Holding its head to one side, the leopard walks away, dragging the dead man beside it, as if he weighed no more than a, than a ... *What?* she asks herself. Then supplies the answer. *Than half a hindquarter of a scrawny white cow.*

Her vision is blurring again. But before the black curtains swing shut, she has a hallucinatory vision of the leopard gathering itself, squatting back on its powerfully muscled haunches, then leaping fifteen feet vertically into a tree with the corpse swinging from its clamped jaws like a rag doll.

And a bird calls. Ku-ku-kuu ... ku-ku-kuu ...

16

THE TEMPLE LEOPARD

M16 held diagonally across his body, Gabriel reached the courtyard where he'd left Eli. He checked all four sides, then looked up at the trees. No bandits. They hadn't struck him as snipers, so he ran in a straight line towards Eli's hiding place. He could see her, but she was slumped over with her neck at an unnatural angle. *Oh, Jesus, don't be dead!*

Just as he reached her, he spotted another AK-47 on the ground. Clearly discarded, but by whom? He reached her a second later and gently lifted her head onto his lap, panting from the exertion in the fierce heat, yet far more concerned with his partner. She was breathing — shallow puffs of air that warmed the back of his hand. He checked her for bullet wounds and relaxed as he found none. He pressed his lips to her forehead, which was burning hot.

Lying her flat, he crawled into the space behind her and retrieved the canteen and his medical kit. He moistened her lips and, when they opened, placed the neck of the canteen against them. Gratifyingly, she sipped some water down. But her eyes remained closed.

"Hey," he said. "Eli. Can you hear me? Come on, Eli. You need to wake up. We have to go."

Her eyes were moving under the lids. As if she were dreaming. Then they fluttered open. He gazed into her grey-green irises as if he could bring her round by sheer will power.

"What are you looking at?" she whispered.

"Thank God. Are you hurt?"

"No. I mean, my knee feels like someone set it on fire, but that's it. He didn't hit me."

"I can give you another shot of morphine."

She shook her head.

"Just some water, please."

Gabriel pressed the neck of the canteen to her lips again and she swallowed greedily.

"Who didn't hit you? I saw an AK, but no body."

"One of Win Yah's men. My gun jammed and he was about to shoot me. Then the leopard just, it came from nowhere. It killed him and jumped into a tree. With him, I mean."

She jerked her chin in the direction of a tall tree, smothered with small, yellow fruits that Gabriel supposed might be unripe limes. He looked up into the branches. At first he saw only the dappled greens and shadows of the leaves. But as his gaze attuned to the patterns of the foliage, he saw it. A patch of dusty yellow-and-black mottling. He followed the curve of the spine and found himself looking into the yellow-gold eyes of the leopard.

The big cat seemed utterly unconcerned at his noticing its lair and blinked slowly without moving. No hissing, no raised hackles, no twitching muscles: it just lay there, one paw dangling over the edge of the thick branch, the other resting proprietorially on the carcass of the dead bandit. Then it bent its head and licked the back of the dead man's neck as if to say, "he's mine now".

"We need to go," Gabriel said. "Can you stand if I help you?"

17

FIRE IN THE HOLE

Win Yah may have been a killer, but he wasn't a stupid killer. He heard gunfire coming from a point somewhere to his right. Then directly in front of him. He recognised both the AKs of his own men and the distinctive chatter of the American M16. Using a prearranged signal, a birdcall, he tried to contact his three subordinates.

"Ku-ku-kuu ... ku-ku-kuu ..."

Had they been alive, they would have responded with a modified version of the same call. Two longs and a short. He waited. Heard nothing. Concluded with regret that they were all dead.

Whoever the woman had brought in to fight alongside her was deadly. And Win Yah knew plenty about deadly fighters. He had lost count of the number of people he himself had sent to their ancestors, both in the service of Pol Pot and on his own account. He'd used guns, machetes, lengths of wood, axes. He'd tortured, beaten and mutilated. Bashed brains out on tree trunks when no weapon was available, or simply to terrify the next person in line. Now he sensed an enemy at least as skilled as he was at cutting the thread that tethered people to their earthly life. And he mumbled one of the few English phrases he knew.

"He who fight and run away, live to fight another day."

Then, not running, but not ambling either, Win Yah quit the Field of Mars.

* * *

Gabriel looked down at the mine he'd retrieved. He didn't want to leave it behind, but carrying it back with him while also helping Eli to walk would be foolish at best, suicidal at worst.

"We need to do something with that. Any bright ideas."

Eli turned sideways and looked at the green-and-black disc. Then back at Gabriel.

"Only the obvious."

Gabriel picked up the mine by its sides and walked away. After a hundred yards, he saw what he needed: a gigantic block of masonry almost as tall as he was. He knelt and laid the mine against the cool grey stone like a plate on display on a dresser. Looking right and left he saw a couple of brick-sized stones and fetched them, wedging them on each side of the mine.

Back with Eli, he retrieved the M16 and set the fire selector to SEMI. He lay on his belly and wriggled into a comfortable shooting position: left arm crooked with the hand cupping the perforated fore end, right hand around the pistol grip, left leg bent at the knee, right straight out behind him. Eli shuffled away from him, pushing herself backwards using her good leg and both elbows.

He settled his cheek against the stock and sighted on the mine's black plastic detonator through the telescopic sight. It was a rookie's target. Solid, stable, face-on. No crosswind. No real possibility of the heat coming off the ground causing the bullet to deviate in flight. No need to worry about its dropping either. Not over so short a range. He closed his left eye and centred the cross-hairs on the detonator. Tightened his finger on the trigger. Inhaled once, and let it out in a hiss.

"Fire in the hole," he murmured.
And squeezed the trigger.

18

THE THIRD MINE

The 5.56mm round left the muzzle with a loud crack. The noise fused with the boom as the mine exploded into a single percussive bang that left Gabriel's ears ringing. He kept his head down, expecting razor-sharp stone chips, or pieces the size of cricket balls, to come spinning towards him. But apart from a light pattering of pea-sized fragments hitting the ground, the mine had done no damage.

He got to his feet and slung the M16 across his back. He gave the daysack to Eli so he'd be able to get to the rifle quickly if he needed to. He braced himself and held his hand out to Eli. She grasped it and pulled herself to her feet. He noticed how she favoured her left leg and hoped she'd manage the long walk back to the pickup.

"Nice shooting, kid," she said.

He smiled.

"Thanks. How are you feeling. Knee OK?"

"I've been better, but I can do this. Come on."

They arranged themselves so that Eli was to Gabriel's left, with her injured leg between them. She hooked her right arm around his shoulder and held him tightly.

He took a step and Eli hopped along beside him. He saw her wince. But there was nothing to be done. He didn't want to give her any more painkillers, wasn't even sure they'd do much good. Within seconds the place where their bodies touched was soaking wet. Eli sighed deeply.

"Fucking hell, Wolfe, I'm sorry I got you into this mess."

He took another step, and helped her match him, holding her round the waist.

"You didn't. Nobody did. Except possibly Win Yah. Shit happens, you know that. We both knew when we signed up for The Department."

Eli grunted out a laugh as she took another halting step.

"Ha! What does he call us? 'My little band of cutthroats'?"

"Yeah, all we need're spotted bandannas round our heads and big gold earrings for the compete pirate look."

It was a lame joke. Barely even qualifying. But it was enough. Eli cracked a smile and they took a few more steps.

They emerged from the courtyard onto the paved path leading away from the temple and back through the forest to the road, the pickup, and salvation. Gabriel was starting to imagine the drive back to the guest house, how he'd tease Eli about being laid low by a cut on her knee.

"Hardly battlefield trauma, was it?" he'd ask. They'd get back to safety and he'd redress her wound, take a look at the burns on her leg, which he realised he hadn't even asked about, then call a doctor. In fact he'd call his boss at The Department. Maybe Don Webster had a contact in Siem Reap who could recommend someone reliable. A couple of ice-cold beers, and maybe a dip in the huge rectangular swimming hole.

Then his toe caught under a root curving up out of the red earth, making him stumble. His left knee collided with Eli's right. Her yell of pain set a covey of birds clattering out of a nearby banana palm, hooting in alarm. Their volume was nothing compared to the shouted stream of oaths issuing from Eli's stretched mouth.

"Fucking HELL, Wolfe, you cunt on a stick, that fucking hurt!"

He started to apologise but the violence of her cursing made him laugh. Her eyes widened and her mouth dropped open.

"I'm sorry, I'm sorry," he said, hurriedly, before the tough Israeli took her anger out on him. "It was an accident."

He did his best to stifle his laughter but he was powerless. Her outraged expression only made matters worse and it was all he could do to stay standing and not drop her on her arse in the dirt. That image set him off again, and it was only the resounding slap Eli delivered to his cheek that startled him into silence.

"First of all, as I said, that fucking hurt, you idiot. Second of all, shut up! There might be more of Win Yah's men still out here."

He sighed out a breath. Shook his head, sending a few droplets of sweat flying to each side.

"Sorry. Again. But I think we're OK. I've been checking around us. I haven't seen or heard a thing. I got two of them and you said a leopard took a third. If there were others, I think they're retreated to regroup. Or just get the fuck away from here. I mean, it hasn't exactly been lucky for them, has it?"

Eli shrugged her shoulders, clearly not mollified.

"Maybe. Maybe not. But I'll tell you one thing."

"What?"

"If you hit my knee again I'll leave you here with them. You can be kitty's next meal."

Gabriel saluted with his free hand.

"Understood. Boss."

"Good. That's better. Now can we please get the fuck out of here? I want a bath, something to eat, a doctor, and a beer. Not necessarily in that order."

They started off again, the world's worst entrants in the three-legged race.

"I'm glad you mentioned the bath," Gabriel said.

"Why?"

"Let's just say you're a little more fragrant than usual."

"You cheeky bastard! Are you saying I stink? I don't know if you've caught a whiff of your own manly aroma recently. It could fell a horse."

19

PRETTY AS A FALLEN MANGO

They bantered their way along the path, falling into a clumsy but serviceable rhythm: step, grip-and-lift, swing, brace, grip, step. Gabriel could feel Eli's hot skin under her shirt but it was more the heat from the sun than an internal fire. Her face was red with the exertion but her eyes were clear and the spots of dangerously high colour on her cheeks had disappeared.

Coming round a curve in the track, Eli stiffened, bringing Gabriel to a stop.

"What the fuck's that?" she asked pointing at a bloody hunk of flesh wedged into a forked branch ten feet above their heads.

"That's the remains of the cow I used to feed the leopard. I startled it off the path and it stepped on a landmine."

"Better it than you, I suppose."

"Yeah, or a kid."

"How many mines did you say there were in Cambodia?"

Gabriel thought back to his conversations with Lina Ly, a Cambodian journalist, and Visna Chey, the hardworking director of the charity *Tom Boh* – Big Brother. Both had helped Gabriel in his quest to avenge the murder of his friend, Vinnie Calder. They had patiently explained to Gabriel the horrific legacy of three decades of war.

"According to the people I spoke to there are five or six million still buried here. Nobody made any maps, even though that's part of the Law of War—"

"Because obviously they were all *massively* concerned about observing the Geneva Conventions."

"So there's one landmine for every three people in Cambodia. Then you've got the unexploded ordnance. Anywhere from two to six million UXOs lying around like fallen mangoes, waiting for a kid to pick one up or an adult to stand on one or disturb it with a plough. All courtesy of those fine upstanding humanitarians and cluster bombing fans, Henry Kissinger and Richard Nixon."

"You sound bitter."

"Me? No, not bitter. But Eli, when we were fighting in uniform, we had to follow the rules, didn't we? We didn't go around shooting civilians, or prisoners. And if there was even a whiff of suspicion, well, just look at Iraq and Afghanistan. Scarcely a day goes by without some poor sod being hauled up before the judge on a charge dug up by a bloody lawyer. But all the time, the politicians are doing whatever the fuck they like. They —"

"Kissinger and Nixon?"

"Yes. Nixon wanted to cut off the North Vietnamese Army's supply lines down the Ho Chi Minh Trail. He practically soaked the whole of Vietnam with Agent Orange and it wasn't working so he asked Kissinger. And Kissinger said, 'OK, Mr President, sir, what I propose is this. We'll just carpet-bomb Cambodia with cluster munitions, even though it's neutral. That ought to do it. Hey! We should mine it too. We could even paint some in pretty colours so kids pick them up to play with'."

Eli held her hands out in front of her, clearly willing to risk a fall if she could turn off Gabriel's rant.

"OK, OK, whoa there, soldier. I get it. Politicians, bad; honest grunts, good. But we're helping put things right here, aren't we?"

Then she stopped talking.

"It's OK," Gabriel said. "You were going to say till you fucked it up, weren't you?"

"Of course! Because it's true. Win Yah should be walking around with a bullet in his brain, but —" She caught Gabriel's look. And smiled, for which he was grateful. "You know what I mean. I missed the shot. That's it."

"So the job's not finished. We stay until it is, OK? But first, and sorry for the soapbox bit just then, we get back to the guest house and get your knee seen to. I meant to ask, how bad are the burns?"

Eli shrugged.

"They hurt, but not as much as the knee. Just superficial, I hope. Or else, the knee is such a fucking wreck that it's drowning out third-degree burns."

"And on that hopeful note, ladies and gentlemen, let's get going again."

20

LEADERSHIP

Win Yah settled himself behind the Jeep's skinny steering wheel. He started the engine, shoved the gear stick into first, and floored the throttle, sending a cloud of red dust whirling high into the trees behind him. On the drive back to camp he rehearsed the speech he would have to give to explain his arrival minus his second-in-command and two of his men.

He was the undisputed boss of the gang he'd named "April 17", from the date the Khmer Rouge took Phnom Penh. But in the drugs and extortion trade in this part of northern Cambodia, "undisputed" was a nuanced term. It might mean "commanding so much respect that none of your loyal foot soldiers would even challenge your choice of music for a barbecue". Or it might mean, "a brutal bully feared by your men only so long as they reckoned there was no stronger candidate to exercise discipline and carry out punishments". He had a pretty shrewd idea which definition fitted him.

By the time he roared into camp, sliding the ancient American all-wheel-drive to a stop outside his hut, he had his speech memorised.

Men came running, gathering in front of the Jeep to hear

what had happened. Some clutched bottles of Cambodia or Angkor beer. One or two were smoking joints. A handful were carrying their AKs. All eyes were on him. He stood up on the bonnet.

"The woman is dead. We tracked her to Jayon Peah temple. She had overpowered Samang and stolen his weapon. Lon Sen wounded her and I killed her myself with this."

He held up his machete, then waited for the cheering and clapping to subside.

"But she was not alone. She had radioed for reinforcements. The Americans. CIA. She called in a helicopter. They were too late to save her. Her head was rolling in the dirt when they arrived. But Lon Sen and your brothers Jey and Dalat were killed. Mown down by a CIA machinegunner who didn't even have the courage to leave the safety of his aircraft."

A barrage of questions erupted. Men were shouting each other down in their efforts to be heard. This was going better than he had expected. He patted the air in front of him and pointed to one of his more loyal soldiers, like he'd seen the Prime Minister's media adviser do at televised press conferences.

"Kiri, what is your question?"

"You are not hurt?"

Win Yah shook his head.

"I was in a cave, dealing with the woman. I was able to return fire without exposing myself to danger. I hit the helicopter many times with my AK, but the damage was done and the Americans fled as soon as I started shooting."

The men muttered among themselves, but Win Yah sensed that he retained control. Now for his killshot.

"It's pay day. Get your vehicles. Go into town and find some beer. And some women."

The men cheered, apparently happy to forget their fallen comrades if money, sex and alcohol were on offer. *Happy like we used to be*, Win Yah mused. *In the good old days*.

21

THE ROAD HOME

Five miles to the east, Gabriel and Eli stumbled out of a clearing onto the track where Gabriel had left the Ranger. For the past five minutes he'd been fighting down feelings of anxiety about the truck. What if it had been stolen? What if someone had slashed the tyres? What if a tree had fallen across it? The fact that he hadn't seen a soul, apart from Win Yah's men, in this part of the country for days did nothing to allay his fears. Nor did the entire absence of trees for a good fifty feet in every direction around the truck.

So it was with a sigh of relief that he nodded at it and spoke.

"Your ride, Milady. America's finest. Four-wheel drive, leather upholstery and AC so cold you'll be wishing you'd packed a sweater."

Eli had been silent for the last few hundred yards and he'd stolen glances at her to see how she was doing, Despite his best attempts to entertain and distract her with stories, jokes and observations about the local flora and fauna, she'd been terse, bordering on non-responsive.

"Just get me in it," she said through gritted teeth.

Holding her tightly round the waist with his left arm, he

retrieved the keys from his pocket and blipped the fob. The door locks opened with muffled clunks and he pulled open the passenger door.

"Here we go. Watch the leg," he said, unnecessarily, as Eli had her gaze fixed firmly on her right knee.

Together, they pushed, pulled, lifted and turned Eli until her bottom made contact with the soft, padded seat. She pulled her right leg in, using both hands to lift and simultaneously protect the swollen joint.

"Oh, fuck that's better," she said, leaning back against the head rest.

Gabriel ran round the front of the truck and climbed in next to her. Offering up a silent prayer, he twisted the key in the ignition, and doubled it when the big V8 caught on the first turn of the starter motor. He cranked the air conditioning dial up to MAX and opened the windows until the fans stopped blowing superheated air out through the vents. Once the air flooding into the cabin was cold, he buzzed the windows closed, selected Drive and manoeuvred the Ranger until he had it facing back the way he'd driven.

"Home, James," he said, patting Eli on her good leg, and accelerated down the dusty red track.

Once he reached the relatively high quality main road, Gabriel put his foot down. At some point on the drive through the forest, Eli had fallen asleep, or had passed out. Whether from heat exhaustion, dehydration, the infection, or a combination of all three, he had no idea. But what he did know was that she needed medical attention. He glanced to his left. Her face was still red, even though the AC had filled the Ranger's cab with air cold enough to raise goose pimples on Gabriel's forearms. Outside the cab, the sky was a sapphire dome that stretched to the horizon in every direction.

To the left, the land was flat, and planted with rows of fruit bushes and banana palms. As soon as CMAC, the Cambodian

Mine Action Centre, cleared land or declared it mine and UXO-free, local people would rush to plant it and begin farming. Regaining the means to support themselves was one of the biggest benefits of demining. That and the freedom from the fear that a walk down a forest path could end up with their losing a limb. To the right, the forest loomed, almost up to the roadside, a thick tangle of palms, deciduous trees and low-growing scrub.

He returned his gaze to the front, and swore.

"For fuck's sake, no! You have to be joking."

22

CHECKPOINT

Three hundred yards ahead, a pickup not dissimilar to his own had been parked diagonally across the road. Standing in the truckbed were two men. They held AK-47s across their skinny chests and wore aviator-style shades whose gold-coloured frames winked in the sunlight. He slowed down as much as he dared without arousing suspicion and looked across at Eli. Her eyes were closed and her breathing was ragged. The M16 rested between her knees.

On the back seat lay the Makarovs they'd collected from the dead bandits and Eli had her right hand resting on the butt of the Sig, which she'd wedged between her thighs. No way would these unofficial toll collectors be willing to let them pass with this amount of firepower on display, however many dollar bills he thrust into their grasping hands.

The men had been thorough in their preparation. On one side of the road, a water-filled ditch crept to within a foot of the tarmac. On the other, a fat-trunked coconut palm had fallen or been dragged to a matching position. No chance for even the most daring of drivers to skirt the impromptu roadblock.

The distance between the trucks had closed to just one

hundred yards when Gabriel made his decision. Letting his right hand slide down and then off the wheel, he took the Sig from Eli's unresisting grip. With twenty yards to go, he stepped on the brake pedal and brought the truck to a stop.

Keeping his foot pressed down hard on the brake, and breathing slowly and deeply though his nose, he waited. He snaked his left arm over the backrest and closed his fingers on the butt of one of the Makarovs, then slid it back. Tucking the barrels of both pistols under his thighs, he thumbed the buttons to lower the windows. The two men in the truck bed were beckoning him to come towards them. He did nothing. They aimed their AKs at the windscreen and started shouting in Khmer. He did nothing.

"If you want my money, boys, you're going to have to come and get it," he murmured.

Eventually, the two men shouldered their AKs and climbed down from the truck bed. They sauntered towards Gabriel, faces grim behind the sunglasses. He waited for them, arms folded, pistols out of sight in his armpits, noting the relaxed postures of the two men as they reached the front of his truck. *You're used to this, aren't you? Is this a revenue stream for you? Do you wait for the tourist coaches to make a real killing? All those fat wallets and Rolexes?*

The man on Gabriel's side stood back a couple of feet from the driver's door and shouted. Gabriel didn't need a translator for this short speech.

"Hundred dollar! You pay now!" He glanced at Gabriel's left wrist. "Watch, too!"

On the other side, the second man was peering in at Eli. He hadn't seen the M16. Yet.

23

ICED

Gabriel uncrossed his arms and stretched them out as if crucified. But the pain coming was all for the two gangsters. Two double-taps to the head put each man on the ground, blood and brain matter spraying out from their shattered skulls.

Leaving the smoking pistols on his seat, Gabriel jumped out of the cab, catching a slight fluttering of Eli's eyelids as he did. He rolled the man on his side into the ditch, then skirted the front of the truck to grab hold of the second man's wrists and drag the body round to join his friend in the stagnant green water. He grabbed the AKs and placed them in the truck bed under a tarpaulin then ran to the gangsters' truck. The idiots had left the key in the ignition. Not used to resistance, Gabriel thought as he swung himself up into the driver's seat and started the engine.

He spun the steering wheel onto full lock and threw the truck backwards towards the banana palm. On contact, he pushed the transmission in Drive and slewed the truck round, narrowly avoiding dropping the front wheel into the ditch, before driving past his own truck and then pulling off the tarmac and nosing the truck into the underbrush.

He climbed down and ran back to the Ranger. Eli was awake.

Her eyes were unfocused though and when he placed the back of his hand to her forehead he could feel the fever burning right out of her skin. He tried to give her some water but the liquid just ran out of her mouth and over her chin.

Nothing for it but to floor the throttle and hope he reached the guest house in time to save her.

Twenty minutes later, Gabriel pulled off the road and onto the rough, stony track that led to the guest house. In front of the two-storey white building two children were playing. They spoke English well enough to hold a conversation, he'd discovered, so he jumped down and ran to them.

"We need a doctor. It is very urgent. Important. Where are your mummy and daddy?"

The little girl straightened. His tone must have impressed her because there was no giggling or sidelong glances at her brother.

"Mummy is inside. I go tell her you need doctor. She telephone Siem Reap."

"OK, good. Good girl. Thank you. *Ah-koon.*"

She clasped her palms together in front of her nose in a hurried *sampeah* and then ran inside.

Gabriel returned to the truck and wrenched the passenger door open. Eli had passed out again. He slid his hands under her thighs and around her back before taking a firm grip and lifting her out of the seat. The M16 toppled sideways and for a moment he worried about the children seeing it, but then dismissed the thought. He swung Eli clear and booted the door shut. With sweat streaming down his face and the inside of his shirt, he carried her up the five wooden steps to the front door, which the little girl had left open and into the mercifully cool interior.

Eli's bedroom was on the ground floor, along a narrow hallway. Reaching the room he bent his knees until he could turn the brass knob and nudge the door open. Finally, he reached the double bed, made up with crisp, white linen as beautifully as any upmarket hotel, and laid Eli on her back.

He racked his brains trying to remember what he'd been taught about infections and fever. *Cool the patient, in an ice bath if necessary*. He snorted at the thought. "Ice! Yeah, right!" he said out loud. Then he gasped as he thought of an answer. The battered red ice cream freezer on the roadside, connected to the house by a snaking blue cable. Jorani, the lady of the house, sold coconuts and cans of Angkor, Coca Cola and Sprite to passing motorists He dashed out of the room, almost colliding with her.

"I called the doctor. He says one hour. Is it Eli?"

"Yes. Her knee is badly infected. She has a fever. We need ice. The freezer?"

Her face, full of concern, lit up with a smile.

"*Jah*! Yes. Lot of ice. Take laundry basket. You fill it!"

Each guest room was supplied with a rattan laundry basket like something from Ali Baba and the Forty Thieves. Big enough for a child to hide inside. As Gabriel and Eli had discovered, laughing, when the owners' four-year-old son had popped up just as they were about to make love under the spinning fan. Gabriel grabbed it, emptied the laundry onto the floor and ran for the front door.

At the roadside, he lifted the dented lid of the freezer, pushed the coconuts and drinks to one side and starting grabbing double handfuls of ice and dumping them into the basket. He was torn between wanting to race back to Eli and staying to collect as much ice as possible. In the end, he compromised. Once he'd half-emptied the freezer, he grabbed the basket by its woven handles and ran back to the house. He stumbled over a discarded length of bamboo scaffold pole left by a careless builder and almost lost his grip on the basket.

Recovering his balance, and keeping up a stream of inventive cursing that his old Regimental Sergeant Major would have approved of, he reached the steps, took them in two strides and was inside the house.

Jorani was sitting on the edge of the bed, pressing a wet flannel against Eli's forehead. She looked up as Gabriel entered the room.

"Eli, she is very hot."

"I know. We need to make her cold with the ice. Help me undress her."

Together they eased Eli out of her clothes. Gabriel used the Böker to cut her trousers off her to avoid harming her injured leg. He sighed when he saw the skin above her knee. It was red and cracked, weeping clear fluid from several fissures.

"Oh, Jesus, Eli. I'm sorry. Hold on. The doc's coming."

Leaving her bra and knickers in place, Gabriel and Jorani laid the laundry basket to Eli's left and gently tipped it up until the ice tumbled out onto the bed with a clicking that would have signalled the cocktail hour in more civilised times. They dragged it around Eli's ribs, neck and head, and scooped handfuls onto her chest. Gabriel fetched a hand towel from the bathroom and wrapped it around a couple of handfuls of ice, then returned to the bathroom to run the improvised cold pack under the tap. This he placed over Eli's forehead, telling Jorani to hold it in place.

"Can you stay with her, please?" Gabriel asked. "I need to do something with the truck."

Jorani nodded vigorously.

"Yes, of course. Go. I stay with Eli."

24

ARMY MAN

Gabriel left the room and went back to the Ranger. The two children had resumed their game at the foot of the steps. Relieved that he wouldn't have to explain to their parents what they were doing playing with a fully automatic assault rifle, Gabriel collected the M16, the Sig and the Makarovs and walked back inside with the mini-armoury clutched to his chest. Now the children did look up.

"You have lot guns," the boy said, his dark-brown eyes wide. "You army man?"

Gabriel smiled.

"Sort of. British army man. I took these from bad men."

The boy smiled back.

"You very brave man."

Inside his bedroom, Gabriel stacked the weapons inside the wardrobe and turned the little brass key before pocketing it. The flimsy lock wouldn't keep a determined thief out, or even a determined child, but he was counting on the absence of a key deterring the owners' children from investigating further. Then he left and knocked gently on the next door along the corridor before entering Eli's room.

"How's she doing" he asked, sitting next to Jorani and looking down at Eli.

"I'm not sure. She breathing better. Head not so hot. But she won't wake up."

As if to prove her point, Jorani patted Eli's left cheek lightly and crooned to her.

"Eliii, Eliii, waaake up, waaake up."

The ice was melting and soaking into the bedlinen. If anything it would help keep her cool, Gabriel thought. He leaned forward and kissed her softly on the lips. And his heart leapt as she returned the pressure, just a little.

"Eli, can you hear me?" he asked, squeezing her hand.

Her lips parted with a tiny *clic*.

"Do you always kiss girls when they're unconscious?"

"Only when they're as beautiful as you are."

"Charmer!"

Her eyelids fluttered open. She focused on Gabriel.

"A beer would be nice," she said.

"Maybe later. How about some water?"

"OK. Water. Then beer."

He fetched a glass from the bathroom and filled it from a litre bottle of Eau Kulen on the night stand. Eli drank greedily this time, runnels of water trickling from the sides of her mouth and onto her chest.

Inwardly, Gabriel was rejoicing. The fever was down. She was going to be all right.

25

TWO SUGARS, ONE CYANIDE

Later, after the doctor had visited, Gabriel and Eli were sitting on the stilted verandah at the rear of the house. It had been built on the side of a hill, so beneath them was thirty feet of clear air. Gabriel was wearing shorts and another Hawaiian shirt, Eli a grey marl vest-top and a turquoise sarong. She'd washed down the tablets he'd given her with water, as instructed. But as soon as his dusty Toyota Camry had turned out of the track and back towards Siem Reap, she'd demanded a beer from Gabriel.

"In fact, bring me two," she'd said, grinning.

Her right leg was propped up on a pink silk cushion on a rattan stool. She'd opened the sarong to her groin so her freshly bandaged knee and cream-smeared thigh were uncovered.

"How are you feeling?" Gabriel asked, after taking a pull on his second beer.

"Not bad, all things considered. The knee still hurts but it's manageable, and I don't know what was in that gunk he put on my burns but they hardly hurt at all."

"Probably some kind of herbal salve. He said they use what the local people have always used, alongside modern medicine."

"Well, he should be selling it all over. He'd make a fortune."

Then she frowned. "Never mind Doctor Phan's Amazing Elixir, what the fuck are we going to do about Win Yah?"

"I was thinking about that on the drive back. We can't risk another ground attack. He'll be expecting it. I'm going to call Don. If he can scare up a plane, I'm going to drop in on Mister Yah from a great height."

* * *

In his office at the army base in Essex, MOD Rothford, Don Webster was staring at a large sheet of paper. Its contents were so dispiriting he was on the point of heading off early for a pre-dinner gin and tonic. Or two. The printed-out spreadsheet in front of him was a patchwork of rectangles highlighted in neon shades of magenta, acid yellow and what he had come to think of as "arrow-poison-frog blue". The screen of his laptop, which was open but pushed to one side, was filled with a document titled, in bold, scarlet, capital letters:

DRAFT REVISED OPERATIONAL PROTOCOLS (FINANCIAL DISBURSEMENTS TO OPERATORS OVERSEAS) – VERSION 17.9

Don leaned back and scrubbed at his closed eyes with his fists.

"Jesus wept! How did I get from commanding 22 SAS to this?" he moaned. Then, louder, "Monica!"

A few seconds later, a woman in her midfifties, elegantly dressed in a dusty pink trouser suit and high-heeled black court shoes stuck her head round his door.

"Yes, Don?"

"Would you pop over to the Armoury and fetch me a Glock 17? Make sure it's loaded, please."

She smiled.

"Hollow-points OK?"

"That would be perfect."

"Going to blow your brains out again?"

"It's these infernal memos from finance, or accounting, or operational directorate six-bloody-teen or whatever they call themselves these days. I don't know, Monica. Can't I just run The Department and hire someone to do," he jabbed his forefinger at the screen, making it tremble on its hinge, "all this?"

"With great power comes –"

"If you say 'great responsibility' I'll shoot myself and then you!"

His PA, used to his theatrical outbursts whenever admin threatened to take over his life, smiled at his joke.

"I think the Armoury's closed for the day. How about a nice cup of tea?"

"Fine. Two sugars, please. And one cyanide."

Monica withdrew and Don forced himself to concentrate on the Word document on the laptop. It was no use. The text was written in a mixture of civil service waffle and sub-military jargon. Since The Department had been overseen by the Privy Council, the number of meetings, memos, reports and the dreaded protocols had multiplied exponentially. His encrypted work phone rang. Thanking whichever God looked after solid combat troops who through no fault of their own had been promoted high into senior management, he looked at the screen. And smiled.

"Hello, Old Sport. I was beginning to think you'd forsaken us. What news on Operation Creek?"

"Not so good, boss. Target's still alive. Eli was captured. She's free now and we killed three enemy but she's hurt. Infected knee wound from a landmine. I need to take the lead on this one and go back to finish the job."

Don switched instantly into ops mode. His favourite.

"Right, Save the debrief for when you're back. I assume Eli's OK?"

"She's fine. She's seen a doctor and her fever's down. He gave her some weapons-grade antibiotics and stitched her up. But she's not really mobile."

"Good. What's the plan?"

"HALO. I need a ride and a chute."

"High Altitude, Low Opening, eh? I seem to remember that was always your favourite jump. That all? Any more firepower?"

"Nope. We're good."

"Leave it with me. I'll make a couple of calls that'll let you bypass security. I'll let you know the wheres and whens once we have the plane sorted."

26

NATIONAL CARRIER

Gabriel's phone rang at ten that same evening. He calculated the time difference: 4.00 p.m. in England.

"Hi, boss. Got me a ride?"

"I tried the Thais, but they're in the middle of a big war games exercise – all their aircraft are committed. However, our friends at British Airways came through, just like they used to. Remember?"

Gabriel had a flash of memory. He and three other SAS men jumping from a modified BA cargo plane – a Boeing 707 – over Helmand Province in Afghanistan at 25,000 feet. Shooting towards the desert like bombs. It was a part of the job he always loved. That sense of freedom, speed and purpose.

"How could I forget? Though I never did get my Air Miles."

"Very droll. You need to be at Siem Reap airport tomorrow at 11.00 a.m. There's a fruit stand about half a mile from the perimeter. Stop there and offload your weapons. The chap manning the stand's one of ours. He'll see your kit gets onto the plane. He'll say, 'do you like local-grown mangoes?' You answer, 'Only if they taste of coconut'. Oh, and try the rice in the bamboo tubes. It's rather delicious. Once you arrive, go to the BA desk and introduce yourself as Mark Light."

In the morning, after having an early breakfast with Eli and telling her to stay in bed, or at the very least to take it easy, Gabriel climbed into the Ranger and headed back towards Siem Reap. Once again, he'd dressed in his tourist disguise of shorts and another loud Hawaiian shirt. This one featured palm trees and parrots.

A leather weekend bag on the passenger seat held a set of camouflage fatigues and a pair of sturdy, sand-coloured combat boots. The weapons, zipped into a canvas kitbag, were in the truckbed under a tarp.

Before leaving, he'd placed a hand gently on Eli's shoulder and looked into those grey-green eyes.

"You OK?"

"I'm fine," she said, smiling. "Jorani told me she used to be a nurse in Phnom Penh. Then she and Borey bought this place and she quit. My only worry is she'll kill me with kindness before you get back. How about you? You ready?"

"Uh-huh. Drop the guns at the fruit stand, go to the BA desk. Pick up my escort. Go to the plane. Jump out of the plane. Find Win Yah. Kill Win Yah. Exfil. Extract."

Eli grinned.

"Easy as falling off a log."

"Or stepping on a mine."

27

DEPARTURE LOUNGE

Two hours later, Gabriel drew up on the side of the road in front of a ramshackle arrangement of trestle tables, umbrellas, plastic chairs and children's toys. Forty feet back from the road, a shack constructed from rough planks and sheets of corrugated iron was all but obscured by palm trees and ferns. Beside it, a white Toyota Corolla was parked under a tarpaulin.

The trestle tables were groaning with mangoes, green coconuts, watermelons and apples. To one side, thick pieces of rice-filled bamboo were grilling over a charcoal fire. To the other, a shiny red moped was parked under an umbrella tied to a length of bamboo cane. A little boy, maybe three or four was playing with a bucket of water round the back of the stand, flicking spoonfuls at a scruffy, yellowish mongrel with swollen teats.

"*Sus'aday, sok sa bai?*" Gabriel said. *Hi. How are you?*

The little boy's eyes opened wide and then he giggled.

"Hello! Hello!" he said.

A movement from the shack caught Gabriel's eye.

A lean man of maybe twenty-nine or thirty ambled out from the doorway and along the path towards Gabriel. He wore loose cotton pyjamas of yellow cotton that gave him an innocent look.

"Do you like local-grown mangoes?" he asked, pointing at a wooden tray of yellow-green fruit that were emitting an intense perfume.

"Only if they taste of coconut."

The man smiled and offered his hand.

"Tran Dhuc."

Gabriel smiled back and shook the proffered hand.

"Gabriel Wolfe. Vietnamese?"

"Half. My Mom's Cambodian."

"I've got some stuff to offload."

"Sure. Let me help you."

Tran lifted the kitbag out of the loadspace as if it weighed nothing. His ropy muscles stood out against his caramel-coloured skin.

"You get yourself on the plane. I'll make sure these are waiting for you."

With the kitbag safely stowed in the Corolla, Gabriel said goodbye to Tran, waved at the little boy, and got back into the Ranger.

"Wait!" Tran shouted.

Gabriel stilled his hand, which was on the point of turning the key in the ignition. Tran poked a paper-wrapped bamboo cylinder through the open window.

"Take this. In-flight food's not up to much, I hear."

Gabriel smiled, said "*Ah-koon,*" and headed on towards the airport.

He parked the Ranger and paid for a week's parking, hoping he wouldn't need it, then grabbed his bag from the passenger seat. The walk from the car park to the departures hall was only a couple of minutes but the temperature had already hit the early thirties and the humidity was oppressive.

Gaining the air-conditioned comfort of the departure lounge, he looked around, getting his bearings. In a far corner he saw the familiar BA logo and strode across the polished floor. At the BA desk, he introduced himself to a dazzling attractive Cambodian woman, dressed in a smart navy jacket, white blouse and red, white and blue scarf.

"Good morning. My name is Mark Light. I believe you're expecting me."

"Good morning, Mr Light. Yes. Your colleague emailed yesterday. Would you please wait for a moment while I call for someone to collect you."

Gabriel nodded his assent and, while the young woman placed a call, took the opportunity to look around at the crowds. Plenty of Chinese and Indians, a few Cambodians, and hundreds of westerners, many of whom wore the cheap, baggy cotton trousers printed with elephants and lotus flowers on sale in Siem Reap market and the dozens of roadside stands selling trinkets. He smiled. He'd overheard a couple in the market at a clothing stall arguing after the man had appeared from behind a curtain, resplendent in an orange and white pair.

Pulling the baggy trousers out sideways from his thighs, the man had asked his companion, "Well, what do you think?"

The woman, late forties, hair pulled back into a bun, lips a vibrant pink, had placed her hands on her hips and stared long and hard at the trousers.

"I think they're lovely." A beat. "But they make you look like a cunt."

Gabriel had laughed out loud, earning a frown from the utterly deflated man, and a complicit smile from the woman.

"Sir? Mr Light?"

Gabriel turned back.

"Yes?"

"Captain Isaacs is on his way to collect you."

28

AIRCREW ONLY

A few minutes later, Gabriel noticed a tall sandy-haired man in a navy pilot's outfit and peaked cap striding through the crowd. He headed straight for Gabriel and shook hands as soon as he arrived.

"Mark, old boy. So good to see you! Come this way."

Gabriel followed Isaacs out of the departure hall through double doors marked "Aircrew Only" and into a grey-painted concrete corridor. Out of hearing of the tourists and, Gabriel imagined, plain-clothes police or anti-terror officers monitoring the travellers, Isaacs turned to Gabriel, without breaking step, and spoke.

"I'm Neil. Hear you're going in for a bit of extreme skydiving."

"Gabriel. And yes. How much do you know."

Neil shrugged.

"Only what I need to know. I'm ex-Royal Air Force, though. Used to fly these sort of runs in Afghanistan from time to time. Big old C-130Js dropping guys out at 20,000 feet, maybe higher depending on what was happening on the ground."

At the far end of the corridor, Neil punched a six-digit code into a keypad, releasing the door and admitting the two men to a huge hangar containing a handful of planes of differing sizes, liveries and states of repair, from takeoff-ready to missing wings or engines.

"Is there somewhere I can change," Gabriel asked. "I feel a tad overdressed for today's activities.

"Really? I thought you looked quite the dandy. Sure," Neil said with a grin. "There's a crew room over there." He pointed to a door to their left.

Gabriel executed a quick costume change, packing his shouty tourist garb into the bag, which he left in a key-operated locker.

Neil led Gabriel between a couple of cargo planes being loaded by forklifts. They emerged into the blinding sun. Heat haze shimmered above the apron, and Gabriel could feel the burning concrete through the soles of his boots. Both men donned sunglasses, Ray Ban Aviators for Neil and orange-lensed Oakleys for Gabriel, secured with a black cloth retainer pushed over the ear-pieces.

Awaiting them on the apron was a Boeing 747 painted in BA's distinctive red, white and blue livery.

"That's us," Neil said.

Inside the plane, Gabriel could see it had been used to make parachute drops before. A rail for static lines had been bolted along one side of the cargo area and a dozen simple metal seats with four-point harnesses had been welded into the airframe each side of the huge rear door.

After making sure the equipment provided was suitable for Gabriel's purposes, including the weapons dropped off by Tran and a couple of additional pieces of kit in a daysack, Neil headed forward to start pre-flight checks.

Gabriel climbed into a khaki flight suit laid out on the floor between the rows of seats and zipped himself in. Next he worked his way into the parachute harness, double- and then triple-checking every buckle and strap. His kitbag lay on the floor. He unzipped it and took out the M16, checked the magazine – full – and brought out the Sig, which he stuck into the nylon tactical holster he'd strapped across the front of the flight suit.

He placed the headphones over his ears and switched on the comms link. Resting on one of the seats was an oxygen bottle and transparent mask. Next to that was a black ballistic helmet with a facemask connected to a second oxygen bottle. He'd need to pre-breathe the pure oxygen for 35 or 40 minutes to flush the carbon dioxide from his system in preparation for the jump. The helmet tank would enable him to survive the radically deoxygenated air outside the plane at the agreed drop altitude of 28,000 feet. He buckled himself in, took the free mask and fitted it over his head.

As the plane took off, Gabriel closed his eyes and concentrated on his breathing. Pure oxygen caused lightheadedness to begin with, but he was expecting it and simply breathed his way through it, repeating one of Master Zhao's old mantras while the gases in his bloodstream adjusted.

"Breathe to where you need it."

29

28,000 FEET

He felt the plane level off, and settled in to wait. Neil had said flying time would be about forty minutes.

"Gabriel? Ten minutes to drop zone," Neil's voice crackled over the radio.

"Thanks. I'm ready."

He removed the headphones and replaced them with the ballistic helmet. He switched breathing masks and tugged on the straps as hard as he could until they were tight against his jaw. No sense losing your air supply just because you didn't want the elastic pinching. He pulled the daysack on across his front. One more check of his harness, including the ripcord on the main and reserve chutes, concluded his pre-jump routine. He held one of the headphones against his ear and waited for final clearance. Neil's voice sounded tinnier through a single can.

"Two minutes to drop zone. We know you have a choice of carriers and we thank you for choosing BA. We strive to make every flight a pleasant one."

Gabriel smiled at the ex-RAF pilot's rote repetition of the corporate boilerplate.

"Thanks, Neil. Maybe a beer and some nuts next time? Out."

The square cargo door opened, admitting a blindingly white beam of sunlight into the dim interior of the plane. Gabriel inhaled deeply, relishing the faintly rubbery smell from the breathing mask. His mind felt as clear as the sky beyond the doorway, which had resolved into a pure blue rectangle.

He patted the Sig and checked the press stud holding the retaining strap in place. The M16 was unwieldy. Normally paratroopers would jump armed with something more compact. A carbine, or a sub-machinegun like the Heckler & Koch MP5K. But beggars can't be choosers.

Gabriel strapped the assault rifle across his chest and walked to the wide-open cargo door. He checked his GPS was working. Don had told him it would be pre-programmed with Win Yah's location. Then he backed up three steps, rocked back and forth on his heel a couple of times, ran ...

... and jumped...

30

HALO

The lenses on his face mask steamed up as the cold air hit them. The roaring of the air past his ears was deafening. Gabriel gasped at the shock of the first half-second of jump-time, then began to adjust as countless hundreds of jumps from his days in the Paras and the SAS jostled for space at the front of his mind.

Settling his arms into a swept-wing configuration, hands arrowing back to his feet, he adjusted his trajectory into a steep, head-down dive and started to enjoy the acceleration towards terminal velocity.

Below him, the forests and farmland of northern Cambodia spread as far as the eye could see in every direction. He knew that, at this altitude, he'd be seeing Thailand, Vietnam and Laos, too.

So many greens, from the bluey shade of eucalyptus to the bright lime-green of the palm trees. Then there were the browns and beiges of the paddy fields. And, in the distance, glinting amid the green like a piece of silvered glass, the Tonlé Sap lake, the largest freshwater lake in Southeast Asia.

He checked his altimeter. 18,000 feet. At 5.6 seconds per thousand feet, he had 90 seconds before the 2,000 feet parachute deployment mark.

Then an unwelcome thought entered his mind.

This was how ex-Delta Force operator Vinnie Calder had entered the afterlife. Shot, then stuffed into the weapons bay of an F-15 and dropped over the Chihuahuan desert in Texas.

The lenses of his face mask had cleared. Gabriel looked left and right. Five hundred yards to his left, a buzzard was circling in a thermal. Gabriel caught the edge of the rising column of warm air and felt it push him up and over. He adjusted his arms and course-corrected as best as he was able, given his airspeed of something approaching 165 miles per hour. He focused on the landing site: an area of farmland he'd identified with Eli. No mines and not too far from Win Yah's compound.

Just a few more seconds of free fall remained to him. He grasped the ripcord handle and readied himself mentally and physically for the abrupt decrease in velocity. He counted down.

"Five thousand ..."

(tighten the grip)

"Four thousand ..."

(squeeze the thighs, knees and feet together)

"Three thousand ..."

(draw in the core)

"Two thousand ..."

(deep breath in)

"One thousand ..."

PULL!

With a sound like a gunshot, the square ram-air parachute burst free of its wrappings and unfurled. The deceleration was intense. As the chute acted as a 200 square-foot air-brake on Gabriel's ten and a half stones, he slowed from 160 miles per hour to something approaching just 17 mph. Despite his physical preparation, he felt his insides lurch painfully as his body rotated through 170 degrees from a near-vertical dive to a head-up orientation.

One minute and 20 seconds after that, Gabriel made landfall. He and Eli had discussed the best approach to parachuting in a country as heavily mined as Cambodia. They'd concluded that the safest landing point would be a road, followed by agricultural land. Farmers wouldn't plant crops on land unless CMAC had either cleared it or declared it mine- and UXO-free.

As the land rushed up to greet him, he pulled down hard on the control line toggles to slow his descent and landed on his feet in the centre of a grove of pineapple trees, crisscrossed with red paths.

31

TWO COMPOUNDS

He gathered the chute into a ball, wound the harness and lines round the unruly bundle of fabric and stuffed the whole lot under a thorn bush. Unlike mines, or the weapons he and Eli had taken from Win Yah's men back in the temple, the parachute could be repurposed into something useful by anyone lucky enough to find it. Gabriel had no qualms about leaving it behind where a child or their parents might stumble across it.

Free of the chute, he shrugged his way out of the daysack and the M16's sling and laid them beside him before unzipping the flight suit and discarding it, together with the helmet and oxygen bottle. He untangled the Sig and its holster and refastened it over his chest. With a full canteen, the Böker, spare magazines for both guns, and the GPS unit, Gabriel Wolfe was ready for the final stage of the operation.

He was three miles from Win Yah's camp. A stronghold surrounded by hundreds of square miles of forest with a single road in and out.

The voice of his dead friend and fellow SAS operator, Mickey "Smudge" Smith, floated back to him down the years.

"Tabbin' cross-country in this heat, boss? Piece of piss."

Gabriel smiled at the memory of the southeast Londoner's jaunty walk as he'd set off with a fifty-pound Bergen and another twenty pounds of weapons and kit through the jungle of Borneo, his deep-brown skin darkened even further with green and black stripes of camouflage makeup.

"Yeah, piece of piss, mate," Gabriel said out loud.

Then he turned to face due south and started walking.

Two hours later, Gabriel reached the patch of forest occupied by Win Yah and his men. Bounded on its northern edge by a river, its eastern by a single-track, red earth road, and its southern and western by fenced-off land with red-and-white CMAC "WARNING! MINES!" signs posted every twenty yards on the trees, the compound spread over roughly three acres. He thought back to the air conditioned briefing room in Whitehall, where, two weeks earlier, he and Eli had stood looking down at a glass-topped, digital map table with The Department's Southeast Asia expert.

* * *

"Unusually for this part of the world, there are very few dangerous animals you'll need to watch out for," she'd said. "There *are* leopards, but they're usually pretty wary of humans. Other than that, no apex predators at all, or none of a size to trouble you two. A few venomous snakes, including King Cobras, but again, you'd have to be extraordinarily unlucky to meet one. No, your main concern is the mines and UXOs."

You got that right, he thought, but without rancour. In truth, anyone with even a passing interest in the history of this beautiful but troubled country would have given him and Eli the same warning.

She'd placed her fingertips about two inches apart on a spot marked with a red dot and slid them apart, zooming in on northern Cambodia, then closer still, until the map revealed roads, rivers and settlements. She leaned across Gabriel to tap a menu icon, and selected 'SATVIEW'. As she withdrew, he caught a faint whiff of her perfume, something deep and musky. The view beneath the glass shimmered and redrew itself.

Now they were looking at a photo of Win Yah's compound itself. Taken by a CIA satellite, the image was so clear Gabriel could see not just individual members of the gang but their weapons and clothing. For a surreal moment, he imagined one of the men moved: he felt if he leaned over and tapped the bandit on the shoulder, he'd look up and wave.

The analyst, Kelly, identified the different buildings and pointed to a hut she said belonged to the warlord himself, Win Yah.

"That's where the target lives." She pointed to a white pickup next to the hut. "That's his ride. A Hilux like they all drive." And a third time, to a rectangular thatched roof. "And that's his armoury. A shitload of AKs, but also shorts that're probably Makarovs or even Tokarevs. We think he may have been running his own little demining operation up there. Not to benefit the local population, I hasten to add. They've cleared land for their own use and have been collecting the mines they didn't need to detonate."

Gabriel listened intently, staring down at the absurdly detailed images in front of him. He registered the intel about the armoury, and about Win Yah's mine clearing efforts. But as Kelly began explaining about which hut belonged to Win Yah, Gabriel's mind flew 5,500 miles southwest to another compound, belonging to another warlord. The Mozambican stronghold of Abel N'Tolo.

Gabriel's SAS patrol was the kill team, assigned the job of killing N'Tolo and retrieving a briefcase of plans. They'd been betrayed at the highest level, way beyond The Regiment's command structure, and Smudge had lost his life. The traumatic events of that failed mission were the trigger point for Gabriel's PTSD and his leaving The Regiment and returning to civilian life.

Not this time, he thought grimly, as he stared at the collection of reed-roofed building comprising Win Yah's base. *Not this time.*

32

M67

As if someone had turned a focus knob in his brain, Gabriel's vision, and his awareness returned from the air conditioned briefing room in London, SW1, to the oppressively hot, humid conditions of the Cambodian forest. He checked the GPS. He was within five hundred yards of the centre of the compound. The track he was using had clearly been made by livestock; dried cowpats drilled with dung-beetle holes marked it every few yards.

Had this been an SAS mission, the approach would have been straightforward. Like the one on N'Tolo's compound was supposed to be, he reflected ruefully. Set up an observation post then sit there for a couple of weeks until you knew what time every single member of the gang took their daily shit and what they used for toilet paper. Draw up the target's schedule. Send in the kill team when he'd be alone and unprotected. Do the business and get out.

Gabriel didn't have that luxury. This was a solo mission. And he didn't have two weeks.

But he did have a plan.

He reached the edge of the compound, keeping low and right on the edge of the track, then skirted the perimeter anti-clockwise, heading for the rectangular hut housing the gang's weapons. His pulse was elevated, but he let it run on, the muscles and the brain needed the extra oxygen. Besides, this was the rush of battle.

All the time he was creeping through the trees and brush protecting the compound, he was straining to catch any sounds that could mean trouble. But the place was quiet. No, not quiet. Silent. *Jesus, I hope they haven't bugged out*, he thought. *We can't screw it up twice.* He steadied himself and took a couple of deep breaths, then a couple of shallower ones. *No. They'll be sleeping. Or stoned. Too hot for mucking about on base.*

The armoury hut was just twenty feet away and, *Thank you, God* backed directly onto the path. Gabriel drew the Böker and stalked nearer until the rough plank wall of the hut gave him cover from the rest of the buildings.

He pried off an eight-inch-wide plank already practically hanging from the rusty nails securing it to the hut's frame and laid it to one side. Peering in, he saw a rack of AK-47s, an assortment of other weapons including a Vietnam-era American M60 machinegun, and a rough shelf laden with a variety of mines, mortar shells and cluster munitions.

The M60 was lying on the ground, easily within reach. Next to it sat an olive green metal ammunition box. Gabriel pulled both towards him. He removed another plank and dragged them out of the hut and back to the shelter of the trees, where he hid them beneath a fallen palm frond.

Back at the armoury hut, he extracted from his daysack one of the extra items thoughtfully provided by the mission quartermaster, and delivered via Tran and Neil. An olive green, spherical, American M67 fragmentation grenade. He removed the safety clip, pulled the pin and let the spoon fly away, then rolled it into the centre of the hut. He turned and ran back fifty yards, finding cover behind a tree.

The grenade exploded and almost immediately the volume of the bang multiplied thirtyfold as the stockpile of mines went up in a burst of detonations that made the air vibrate. The small arms ammunition started exploding next, adding their insane chatter to the ruckus. Fragments of burning wood and reed thatch filled the air, along with the smell of detonated TNT. Gabriel readied himself. Curled his finger round the M16's trigger. Checked the fire selector was set to AUTO.

He counted.

One.

Two.

Three.

And ran forward.

Any stoned bandits out in the open would meet a hail of bullets. No quarter given.

But only one man had rushed out into the centre of the compound.

A man Gabriel recognised from photos.

A man masterminding the Cambodian end of a complex drugs-for-cash-for-weapons smuggling route through Thailand and on into the Gulf states, Saudi Arabia, Lebanon and Syria.

A man he was here to kill.

He raised the M16 to his shoulder and fired.

33

M16

Win Yah had never minded not having his men around him. He preferred it that way. It gave him time to think. Time to reflect on the future. In particular, how to find a way to make one, final, life-changing deal with the Thais and buy his way to the West.

His men would be gone for at least another day. You could buy a lot of loyalty with a few hundred dollars in this part of the world. Not that he knew any other. A couple of days' drinking, gambling, whoring and fighting, and when the money was gone, back they'd come, fired up and ready to follow his orders without question.

In the early days he'd been happy to deliver punishment beatings, amputations or summary executions for disobedience. But like many leaders before him, he'd discovered – slower than most, admittedly – that often, carrots were more effective motivators than sticks. Even sticks with four-inch nails hammered through the business end.

Just as he was musing on his good fortune in surviving for so long, a huge explosion shattered the calm. He rushed out of his hut to see what had until a few seconds ago been his armoury reduced to a blackened patch of ground below a roiling black cloud of smoke. But the sight of the devastation, and the random pops and whines of exploding ammunition, weren't what attracted his attention.

It was the lone figure, carrying an M16 assault rifle, standing in the centre of his compound.

Win Yah hadn't survived four years under Pol Pot's murderous reign, the ensuing invasion by the Vietnamese, and years of bloody civil war without developing a finely tuned sense of self preservation. Even as his eyes locked onto the intruder's, he was already turning away. He carried a pistol, more of a status symbol than the AK-47s, which any kid could get hold of if they wanted to, but he didn't bother using it.

Someone, probably a rival warlord, had sent someone to kill him. Well, they'd regret it very soon. But right now, he needed to get away and regroup before killing the assassin.

The bullets from the assault rifle snapped past his ears like hornets, but he was small, lithe and very fast and as he reached a path winding through a group of small huts he knew he was safe.

Beyond the huts was the forest. Without telling his men, Win Yah had cleared his own, personal escape route. Over the years, he had extended the track for half a mile until it met the metalled road. Buried in the bush was a second Toyota Hilux pickup, gassed up and ready to go, with the key resting on top of a rear tyre.

He ran down the track now, rehearsing the sequence of movements that would get him safely inside the cab and cheating death once more.

34

THE FOURTH MINE

Even though the M16 was set to fully automatic fire, Gabriel didn't go crazy, spraying the whole magazine at the target in a couple of seconds. But the man was fast. He must have been ready for an attack at any time, so hadn't wandered out into the compound, staring around him in shock and waiting to be gunned down. Instead he'd set off like a startled antelope, turning and twisting as he ran and evading Gabriel's bullets. Gabriel, fearing his man would escape into the dense forest, stopped running, aimed more carefully and fired a short burst at Win Yah's back.

Win Yah screamed as the 5.56mm rounds tore into the soft flesh of his right buttock and thigh. Blood and tissue erupted from the impact points as the rounds blew up wound cavities inside his muscles. He stumbled and lurched leftwards off the path.

What happened next seemed to happen in slow motion.

He staggered a few steps and stuck his hand out to steady himself against a narrow tree trunk. Little more than a sapling, really.

His right leg, now soaked with blood from hip to shin, was dragging but he came down hard on his left.

Gabriel saw a small cloud of bluish-grey smoke and a yellow-white flash. He heard a sharp, percussive pop.

Something green and cylindrical, the size of a tin of baked beans, jumped up in front of Win Yah.

Gabriel dived to the ground, smacking hard into the hard-packed red earth.

The cylinder reached the top of its ascent when it was level with Win Yah's midriff.

Then it exploded.

Gabriel heard the fragments of metal whistle through the air above him. Heard Win Yah's scream. And the thump as his body toppled to the ground.

He jumped to his feet and ran towards the fallen warlord.

The mine was a Russian-made OZM-3 "bounding" model, aka a "Bouncing Betty". It had been designed to jump up to roughly waist-height before the main charge detonated. Win Yah's abdomen had been ripped open, and a slithering mass of viscera – purplish-silver, yellow, dark red – had tumbled onto the ground. Blood was jetting from the severed aorta and flowing from his mouth, nose and ears.

The man would bleed out in under a minute, but Gabriel pulled the Sig from its holster and shot him between the eyes. Then he walked back the way he had come. Feeling nothing but a sense of accomplishment. Bringing death to those who deserved it was a hell of a lot different from being the unwitting fool who opened the door and let it in to the lives of those who didn't.

The task was complete; the mission wasn't. The warlord was dead and his materiel destroyed. But the men who had terrorised and extorted the villagers in this part of Cambodia would simply elect a new leader and carry on as before. Gabriel had no intention of letting that happen.

He reached the compound's eastern fringe. The place was still deserted. Despite the recent destruction of the armoury, the forest was already filled with birdsong, monkey calls and the incessant chittering buzz of millions of insects.

He walked to the tree behind which he'd hidden the M60 and

lifted the machinegun by its carrying handle. With the metal box of ammunition belts in his other hand he trotted over to Win Yah's hut. There, he set up the M60 on an upturned Angkor Beer crate, spreading the legs of the bipod wide and settling the feet on the soft wood. He fitted a 100-round ammunition belt through the feedway and released the safety lever. Ready to fire.

Then he settled his back against the door post. And waited for the dead warlord's gang to return to base for the last time. What would the politicians back in the UK say if they knew he was here, primed to kill a couple of dozen Cambodian bandits in cold blood? No prisoners taken. No warning shouted. What would the media say? The human rights organisations? It didn't matter. They were there and he was here.

Since joining The Department, Gabriel had seen too much of the evil that men – and women – did to care about the chatter around posh London dining tables. Let the journalists, the lawyers, the activists and the politicians condemn, call for greater supervision, start petitions, write open letters to the papers, and revel in the whole rigmarole of liberal handwringing. Out here, in a country still reeling from thirty years of war, where the men now in charge had once filled their days bashing babies' brains out against trees and marching their parents off to the killing fields, the reality was simpler, starker, and, at times, more brutal.

He thought of Lina Ly again. The journalist had shared a little of her background with him during his previous visit to Cambodia. The story of her escape from the genocide while the Khmer Rouge were marching her entire family off to be murdered had stirred something inside him.

Every soldier knows of massacres. Some are taught at staff colleges as lessons on obeying the Law of War, like My Lai in Vietnam and Srebrenica in Bosnia. Others are perhaps witnessed and never spoken about. Only to rear their fearful heads in nightmares from which men wrench themselves, sweating and crying to be held, if they're lucky, by their wives or girlfriends, or if not, in the soothing embrace of whatever alcohol they keep under the bed. But to meet someone, to share a bed with someone, who had come so close to extermination, to hear her dry-eyed recounting of the tale while trying to imagine a young girl's raw terror ... that made the statistics of genocides past and present real.

The men he was waiting for might have been pressed into service, or they might have joined the Khmer Rouge willingly. It didn't matter. Not to Gabriel. Not now. They had become killers. Murderers. Now they were terrorising a new generation of Cambodians. And they would start to recruit them and pass on their trade. He had to break the chain.

35

M60

He slept when the sun went down, briefly turning the sky a deep orange, and awoke at dawn. Leaving his post only for the minimum necessary, he waited on, constructing a makeshift shelter out of a section of thatch from the hut's roof when the sun was at its height.

At 2.25 p.m. a swell of competing male voices from the other side of the compound jerked him out of a daydream. Win Yah's men were returning.

Later ...

... when the last, spinning, 7.62mm cartridge case had plinked to the ground to join the hundreds of its fellows that lay scattered all around Gabriel ...

... when the M60's snarling roar had fallen silent ...

... when the screams had ended ...

... when the red-hot barrel had begun to cool ...

... when the sharp tang of burnt propellant and hot brass had dispersed a little ...

... when the cloud of blue-grey gunsmoke had spread upwards into the tree canopy to create a cage of sunbeams around the compound's central yard ...

... Gabriel got to his feet.

His back was sore and his hands and wrists felt as though an electric current were running through them. His ears were ringing. His nose itched. And throughout his body, in every muscle, every organ, every bone, vein, artery and nerve fibre, the adrenaline ran like a drug.

The compound reeked of blood. Two dozen bandits lay dead, their bodies torn apart by the destructive firepower of the M60. Gabriel stood for a while, surveying the charnel house he had created, wondering whether feelings of self-loathing, disgust or shame would come knocking at the rear doors of his consciousness.

The doors remained undisturbed. He had done what he had come to do.

Apart from a few new scratches and dings where pieces of the exploding armoury had hit it, Win Yah's Hilux was in perfectly driveable condition. Thirty minutes later, Gabriel was driving back towards the guest house at a very law-abiding 50 mph. The truck bed housed an impressive collection of automatic and semi-automatic weapons beneath a pile of timber. Gabriel had a simple plan if he encountered any cops. Out with the wallet. Pay the *saamnauk*. No haggling.

In the event, he reached the safety of the guest house without encountering anything more inconvenient than a farm trailer loaded with an entire family, plus two dogs and a scrawny white cow. He wanted desperately to see Eli, but the weapons were his first concern.

He drove past the house and down the gravel track to the swimming hole. "Hole" was a poor term to describe the rectangular artificial lake the size of an Olympic swimming pool fed by an underground spring. Jorani had warned him and Eli on the first day about the swimming hole. The end near the thatched cabanas where guests could eat or swing in the hammocks was only three metres deep, but at the far end, where the track curved round the pump house, it dropped to seven.

It was here that he pulled up. After unloading the timber, he took the weapons, the longs and the shorts in turn, and flung them out over the opaque green water, beginning with the M60. Forty times he repeated the sequence of moves until it attained an almost graceful rhythm. Forty times he rid Cambodia of another killing machine. Forty times a Kalashnikov, a Makarov or a Tokarev splashed into the water to sink for ever. Put beyond use, unless bottom-dwelling creatures could lay their eggs beneath them or inside their barrels.

Back at the house, he pushed open the front door and entered the blissfully cool air-conditioned interior.

"Eli? Jorani?" he called.

36

HONOUR IS MINE

The children came running. Grinning widely, they shouted "Hello, hello! How are you?" before taking his hands in theirs. Chattering away in a mixture of English and Khmer, they led him along the corridor and down a short flight of steps, to the conservatory at the rear of the house.

And there, occupying two brass-bound teak steamer chairs, sat Eli and Jorani. Cream blinds shaded them from the late afternoon sun. A ceiling fan cooled them.

The two women had tall glasses beside them on rattan tables. Glasses filled with a pale-green liquid and stuffed full of ice cubes and mint leaves. They both looked up as the children announced his arrival in excited voices. Jorani stood and embraced Gabriel. Then dipped her head and slid past him.

Eli smiled at Gabriel, a thousand-watt expression that he knew he could never live without.

He leant down and kissed her on the forehead. It was warm, not burning. He lingered there while he inhaled her scent: lemon, clean skin and something herbal from the burn salve.

When he straightened, Eli spoke.

"What took you so long?"

"Tidying up loose ends."

Eli grinned.

"Paperwork, you mean? Filling in expenses forms?"

"Something like that."

Gabriel and Eli met on the rear deck at 9.00 p.m. to find Jorani and Borey drinking Angkor beers. Together, the quartet looked out over the thousands of square miles of forest stretching before them, lit by a full moon that rendered the trees a pewter grey.

Gabriel stared up at the moon. He closed his eyes and inhaled the fragrance of the forest, which mingled with the lemongrass, ginger and garlic aromas wafting out from the kitchen. What had Master Zhao said about how to live your life?

"Live your life today. Do not look back, for the past is unchanging. Do not look forward, for the future is unknowable. Be here, now. Do good, now."

I hope I do, Master, he said silently. *I hope you would be proud.*

And a voice whispered to him on the breeze from the east.

Always, Wolfe Cub. Always.

The End

COPYRIGHT

ACKNOWLEDGMENTS

There are a few people I want to thank for helping make this book possible and for supporting me in my writing.

My dear friend and yoga teacher, Clare Allen, for inspiring me to write this story.

Ponheary Ly and Lori Carlson for allowing me the great privilege of visiting their school in Koh Ker, Cambodia, to chat to the kids there and see a little of their lives. (Helping make and serve the school lunch was fun, too.)

My fellow yogis for showing such love and friendship on our trip to Cambodia: Sarah Bennie, Lisa Blood, Sharon Bright, Dawn Brown, "Big" Mike Cole, Daisy Allen Crook, William Crook, Sarah Hunt, Millie James, Kate Jermolova, Clive Nash, Gaenor Nokes, Liga Piraga, Tanja Schleipen, Gina Suddaby, Vicci Sutton, Ginny Tobias, Nikki Urquhart and Paul Urquhart.

You for buying this book. Every penny of the royalties goes to the Ponheary Ly Foundation.

Jo Maslen and Sandy Wallace, my skilful and diplomatic first readers.

My editor, Michelle Lowery, from whom I have learned so much about how to make a book better.

My proofreader, John Lowery, who coined the phrase "proximity alert", which I love.

Simon Alphonso, OJ "Yard Boy" Audet, Ann Finn, Yvonne Henderson, Vanessa Knowles, Nina Rip and Bill Wilson for being my "sniper spotters".

My advanced readers for picking up any last-minute editorial glitches.

And my family, as always, for being the centre of my world.

Andy Maslen
Salisbury, 2018

ALSO BY ANDY MASLEN

The Gabriel Wolfe series

Trigger Point

Reversal of Fortune (short story)

Blind Impact

Condor

First Casualty

Fury

Rattlesnake

No Further (coming soon)

The DI Stella Cole series

Hit and Run

Hit Back Harder

Hit and Done

Blood Loss: A Vampire Story

Non-fiction

Write to Sell

100 Great Copywriting Ideas

The Copywriting Sourcebook

Write Copy, Make Money

Persuasive Copywriting

ABOUT THE AUTHOR

Andy Maslen was born in Nottingham, in the UK, home of legendary bowman Robin Hood. Andy once won a medal for archery, although he has never been locked up by the sheriff.

He has worked in a record shop, as a barman, as a door-to-door DIY products salesman and a cook in an Italian restaurant. He eventually landed a job in marketing, writing mailshots to sell business management reports. He spent ten years in the corporate world before launching a business-writing agency, Sunfish, where he writes for clients including *The Economist*, Christie's and World Vision.

As well as the Stella Cole and Gabriel Wolfe thrillers, Andy has published five works of non-fiction on copywriting and freelancing with Marshall Cavendish and Kogan Page. They are all available online and in bookshops.

He lives in Wiltshire with his wife, two sons and a whippet named Merlin.

YOU'RE HELPING GIVE KIDS IN
CAMBODIA A FUTURE.

I am donating all my royalties for this book to the Ponheary Ly Foundation.

Some readers have also donated directly. You can add your donation through my JustGiving page.

AFTERWORD

To get a free copy of Andy's first novel, *Trigger Point*, and exclusive news and offers, join his Readers' Group at www.andymaslen.com.

Email Andy at andy@andymaslen.com.

Follow and tweet him at @Andy_Maslen.

Join Andy's Facebook group, The Wolfe Pack.

Made in the USA
Monee, IL
10 April 2021